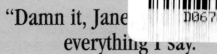

"Damn it, Jane... everything I say."

He was right outside her door. She didn't want him to hear her crying.

"Jane, please, listen to me."

Her head flew up at the sound of his voice, no longer muffled by the door.

"Oh, Jane."

He moved to sit beside her on the bed and wrapped her in his arms. She wanted to resist but found it impossible. His gentle hands cradled her head against his strong shoulder. "All I seem to do is make girls cry," he murmured.

Jane sniffed, trying to control her tears. She didn't like her broken heart being compared to a young girl's tantrum, but she couldn't think of any scathing retort.

"How can I prove I love you?" he whispered.

She could guess what he considered proof. The last thing she wanted him to know was that she longed for that "proof" every night...!

Dear Reader,

'Tis the season to be jolly, and Harlequin Historicals has four terrific books this month that will warm your heart and put a twinkle in your eye!

Cassandra Austin's new book, *Heart and Home,* is very aptly named this holiday season. Known for her raw, emotional Westerns, Ms. Austin stays true to her style with this story of starting over and finding true love. Physician Adam Hart vows to start a new life in Kansas, hoping that his "society" fiancée will eventually join him. But as his feelings for his beautiful, caring neighbor grow, the young doctor finds his ideas of love transformed....

Don't miss our special 3-in-1 medieval Christmas collection, *One Christmas Night.* Bestselling author Ruth Langan begins with a darling Cinderella story in "Highland Christmas," Jacqueline Navin spins an emotional mistaken-identity tale in "A Wife for Christmas" and Lyn Stone follows with "Ian's Gift," a charming story of Yuletide matchmaking.

If you want a Regency-era historical tale that will leave you breathless, don't miss *A Gentleman of Substance* by Deborah Hale. Here, a taciturn viscount offers marriage to the local vicar's daughter, who is pregnant with his recently deceased brother's child. And in *Jake Walker's Wife,* a Western by Loree Lough, a good-hearted farmer's daughter finds her dream man in the Texas cowboy hired on—only, he's wanted by the law....

Enjoy! And come back again next month for four more choices of the best in historical romance.

Happy Holidays,

Tracy Farrell,
Senior Editor

Please address questions and book requests to:
Harlequin Reader Service
U.S.: 3010 Walden Ave., P.O. Box 1325, Buffalo, NY 14269
Canadian: P.O. Box 609, Fort Erie, Ont. L2A 5X3

HEART and HOME

Cassandra AUSTIN

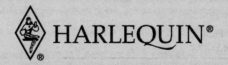

HARLEQUIN®

TORONTO • NEW YORK • LONDON
AMSTERDAM • PARIS • SYDNEY • HAMBURG
STOCKHOLM • ATHENS • TOKYO • MILAN • MADRID
PRAGUE • WARSAW • BUDAPEST • AUCKLAND

ISBN 0-373-29090-X

HEART AND HOME

Copyright © 1999 by Sandra Detrixhe

Visit us at www.romance.net

Printed in U.S.A.

Books by Cassandra Austin

Harlequin Historicals

Wait for the Sunrise #190
Trusting Sarah #279
Cally and the Sheriff #381
Hero of the Flint Hills #397
Flint Hills Bride #430
The Unlikely Wife #462
Heart and Home #490

CASSANDRA AUSTIN

has always lived in north-central Kansas, and was raised on museums and arrowhead hunts; when she began writing, America's Old West seemed the natural setting. A full-time writer, she is involved in her church's activities as well as the activities of her three grown-to-nearly-grown children. Her husband farms, and they live in the house where he grew up. To write to her, send a SASE to: Cassandra Austin, Box 162, Clyde, KS 66938.

Dedicated to my sisters:
Nora, Sally, Nancy, JoAnn, Bobbie and Mari.

Special thanks to Warren S. Freeborn, Jr.,
our retired family doctor and friend, for assistance
with medical aspects of this book.
Any errors that remain are purely my own.

Chapter One

Kansas, autumn, 1879

Dr. Adam Hart leaned against the unyielding back of the train seat. He had almost reached his destination; his chance to practice medicine in the Wild West was a few short miles away.

Only one thing kept him from feeling completely elated. He reached into the inside pocket of his suit coat and withdrew the letter Doreena Fitzgibbon had given him just before he boarded the train. "Don't open it until you're underway," she had whispered. He had hugged her and kissed her and promised yet again to send for her once he was settled.

He didn't read the letter now, but tapped a corner of it thoughtfully against his chin. She wasn't coming west. "I'm confident," she'd written, "that once you have served the year you must in that backward town, you will come home and we can be married."

Hadn't she listened to his descriptions of this land? Didn't she recognize the wonderful opportunities that were here? Wasn't she as eager as he to live surrounded by the unspoiled prairie?

Evidently not. Perhaps he had made the whole adventure sound a little *too* exciting. And the gunfights. He should never have mentioned the gunfights.

At least, he thought with a sigh, she had given him a year. The glowing reports he'd send home were bound to win her over, then she would consent to move here and become his bride.

The train slowed for the Clyde, Kansas, station, and Adam strained to see out the dirty window. A crowd had gathered on the platform under a banner that read Welcome Dr. Heart.

Adam grinned. He could ignore the misspelling with a greeting like this. As the train pulled to a stop, a brass band started playing…something. It was hard to tell what since the musicians were hardly together. Still, Adam was warmed by the sentiment. He gathered the two bags he had with him, stepped into the warm autumn air and received a rousing cheer from the crowd.

A rather stout man who couldn't have been much more than five feet tall stepped away from the others, motioning them to silence. "George Pinter, at your service," he said as the band tapered off. "Mayor of this fair city."

"Mr. Pinter," Adam said, "this is indeed a warm welcome."

Pinter beamed. "My buggy is waiting to take you on into town," he said, directing Adam along. "Your trunks will be delivered straight away."

Adam climbed in beside the little man and they started toward the main part of town, a few blocks away. The band struck up again and the crowd followed.

"We have a house for you to live in that should serve well as an office besides," Pinter shouted over the noise. "I'd suggest you eat next door at the Almost Home Boarding House. Miss Sparks sets a fine table."

Somehow the particulars of living and eating had not occurred to Adam. He had always pictured Doreena keeping house. "Until my fiancée arrives, I might do that," he shouted back.

The buggy stopped in front of a tidy little two-story frame house with a narrow porch nestled between currant bushes. As Adam stepped out of the buggy, he noticed the house next door, a much larger affair with a porch that wrapped around two sides. A few late flowers bloomed in the flowerbeds beside the steps. That house, he realized, would suit Doreena much better than his tiny one.

He shook off the thought. When Doreena came west, it would be because she loved him. Where they lived was immaterial.

Pinter had opened the front door and was waiting

for Adam to join him. The house had obviously been scrubbed clean. Adam walked across the front room, furnished with a desk and a few mismatched chairs, and peeked into what looked like a well-appointed kitchen.

Turning back into the room, he discovered that several of the townspeople had followed them in. More crowded the porch and street outside. The band began another tune.

"There's a bedroom here you could use for examinations," Pinter shouted, indicating a door. "Upstairs is another. Don't worry about dinner tonight. I'll be over to get you."

Adam thanked him, setting the two bags on the desk.

"Well, come along, folks. Let's let him get settled. Your trunks'll be along."

Pinter shooed everyone out. Adam followed, closing the door behind them. He then turned and leaned against it, closing his eyes. His dream of practicing medicine on the frontier was about to come true. The perfection of the moment was marred by a touch of melancholia. It might have been homesickness, but he was inclined to think Doreena's letter was the cause.

He was reminding himself that Doreena would come around when suddenly the door behind him shook with someone's forceful knocking. He swallowed a groan at the abuse to his shoulder blades and flung open the door. He wasn't sure what he had expected. The mayor again, perhaps, or the men who had promised to bring his trunks.

What he found was a tall young woman who seemed as surprised to see him as he was to see her. She was covered from neck to toe in a simple dress of blue calico dotted with brown flowers. Her dark brown hair was pulled savagely back from her face and bound at the nape of her neck. A few wisps of hair had escaped their confinement and curled around her face, softening the effect quite charmingly. Dark circles around her brown eyes made them seem too large for the pale face.

"I'm sorry to bother you," she said. "I was looking for Dr. Hart."

"You've found him," he said, stepping aside and opening the door wider. She remained standing on the porch.

"You're…younger than I expected." She waved a hand as if deciding that was unimportant. "Grams is quite ill," she said. "Can you come see her?"

"Your grandmother?" Were they both ill, or was this exhaustion he saw in the young woman's face? Adam moved quickly to the desk and grabbed the smaller of the two bags. He joined her on the porch and closed the door.

"I'm Jane Sparks," she said, leading the way. "I run the boardinghouse next door."

In a moment they were inside the large house. She led him past a tidy parlor, through a dining room and into the kitchen. The smells that greeted him told him her dinner preparations were well underway.

She led him into a tiny room just off the kitchen. A narrow bed took up most of the available space. A woman Adam guessed to be in her sixties lay covered to her neck with a white sheet. As they entered, her body was racked with an agonizing cough. The granddaughter hurried to her side, supported her shoulders and held a handkerchief until the spell passed.

"Pneumonia," Adam whispered. He didn't need to see the pale skin and overbright eyes, or touch the hot dry brow. He could hear it in the sound of her breathing and the dreadful cough.

"Yes, I thought so," Miss Sparks said. She showed him the blood on the handkerchief before she tossed it aside. She dipped a clean cloth in a basin of water, wrung it out and smoothed it carefully on the fevered brow. She must have left this task only a few minutes before. "Is there anything you can do for the pain?"

Adam set his bag on the edge of the bed across from Miss Sparks and found his stethoscope. He needed to know how far the infection had developed. He listened to the rattle in the woman's lungs while the granddaughter made soothing sounds.

"When she's awake, she's in such pain it breaks my heart. I just want her to sleep."

The last was spoken just above a whisper. The

emotional and physical strain the young woman was under was clearly visible.

"I could give you something to help you rest," he suggested gently. "You could find someone else to care for her."

She didn't look up from her task. "I can't," she said. "I have to be here."

Adam slipped the stethoscope back into his bag. "Her lungs are full of fluid," he said. "My recommendation is to drain them."

"Drain them?" The dark brown eyes turned in his direction and he was struck again by how large they were.

"With a tube, uh, into the chest cavity." Adam touched his own side. He knew it sounded pretty awful. Well, it *was* pretty awful. But he had seen it done successfully, and he knew he could do it. "She's drowning, actually, in the infection."

"This would…hurt her?"

"There would be some pain, yes, but she's in pain now, and it could save her life."

The young woman shook her head and turned her gaze back to her grandmother. "I can't let you hurt her."

"I don't mean to hurt her," he said. "I want to save her. If I don't do it, she will die. It's her one chance."

Tears welled up in Miss Sparks's eyes and she brushed them away. "Don't you understand? It's already hopeless, and she's already had more pain than she can stand—than *I* can stand.''

Adam clinched his teeth as the dying woman took another rattling breath. ''Is there other family I can talk to?'' he asked.

''No. We only have each other.'' She turned to him and spoke fiercely for the first time. ''I won't let you experiment on Grams. If you can't help her sleep, then there's nothing you can do.''

Adam hesitated. This wasn't how he had imagined starting his practice. He had planned to save his patients. Especially the first one. ''Miss Sparks, you don't need to be afraid of modern medicine. I'm a trained physician. I want—''

''Thank you for coming, Doctor. I'm sorry I bothered you. If you'll just tell me what I owe you...''

She had dismissed him. She returned the cloth to the basin, repeating a task she had doubtless done a thousand times. He watched her for a moment, then found the bottle of morphine. He poured a tiny measure of the powder into a folded paper and crimped the edge closed.

Handing it to her, he told her the price and said, ''Dissolve this in a little water and see if she can drink it. I don't think you'll need more than that.'' He hoped she understood the last as his prediction on how much longer she'd have to nurse her grandmother.

She reached for it cautiously. As soon as it left his fingers, he turned from the room. She caught up with him in the kitchen and paid him the money without another word.

He made his way back through the dining room and down the hall, wondering who would finish preparing the meal while she waited for the old woman to die. He knew he shouldn't be angry with Miss Sparks. She thought she was protecting her grandmother. Still, he couldn't help thinking that a dramatic rescue of such an ill patient would have gotten his practice off to a better start.

Jane returned to her seat beside Grams just as she heard the front door close behind Dr. Hart. What had she expected? That the doctor would tell her Grams wasn't dying, that everything would be all right? Had she expected him to offer a miracle cure the other doctors had not?

She shook her head. Of course not. Grams had taken ill almost three months ago and had been unable to leave her bed now for several weeks. Even if she survived the pneumonia, she would never be well. Dropsy, the doctors had said. Her heart was failing.

All Jane had expected from Dr. Hart was something that would stop the pain when Grams awoke. Every breath was agony for her grandmother, and all she could do was cry.

Jane fingered the paper in her hand. That was what he had given her, something for the pain. Then why did she feel cold inside?

Because he had put it into words. Grams was dying. Not in a few months but now. And he had forced her to make the choice to let her.

"Oh, Grams," she whispered. "Did I do the right thing?"

When she thought of the doctor poking a hole in Grams's frail side, forcing a tube into her chest cavity, which hurt already, Jane knew she had been right. She had to believe she was right.

She refreshed the cloth on Grams's forehead one more time, then went back to the kitchen. With the door open she could hear nearly every breath her grandmother took. It had become the rhythm of her life these past few days, the slow labored inhale and exhale. With both dread and longing she waited for the moment when the breathing would stop. How could Grams take much more of this? And how could she?

Adam's trunks arrived shortly after he returned. He set to work unpacking them immediately, glad for the activity. The steady stream of patients he had imagined didn't materialize. He checked his front door a couple of times and finally left it open so he'd be sure to hear a knock. All the time he was upstairs he listened for a voice from below. He opened the windows, thinking he might hear footsteps on his porch. He finished unpacking and returned to the front room, having been uninterrupted the entire time.

Uninterrupted if he didn't count his own thoughts. He kept seeing Jane Sparks with tears in her eyes and that poor woman lying beside her.

He could have saved her. He still could. There was probably still time. But how would he convince the granddaughter? She hadn't been willing to consider the procedure. And he didn't know how to convince her.

If he were more experienced, had seen a little more death and had saved a few more people, he would know what to say. But he didn't, and his first patient in his new home was going to die, probably within the next few hours.

He was pacing the front room, seething with guilt and frustration, when he finally heard footsteps on his porch. He turned toward the open door to find Mayor Pinter there.

"Evening," the little man said. "Did you get settled in?"

"Pretty much," Adam said, forcing a smile. "I hadn't realized it was dinnertime already."

"We eat a mite earlier here than in the city, I suppose."

"I won't complain about that," Adam said, realizing how hungry he was. Wonderful smells had been wafting through his open windows and door all afternoon, smells he had tried his best to ignore because he knew they came from Miss Sparks's kitchen.

"It's nice of your family to let me come to dinner,'' he said, slipping into his suit coat as he joined Pinter on the porch.

"I don't have a family," Pinter said, preceding Adam down the steps. "I take breakfast and dinner at the boardinghouse. Got myself a permanent seat at her table. I recommend you do the same. Unless you got talents I don't know about, it'll likely be the best food you're gonna find.''

The boarding house. So much for putting Miss Sparks out of his mind. Not that he would have anyway, Adam supposed, but he had been looking forward to a distraction.

"Miss Sparks has got four rooms upstairs that she rents out. If they're all filled, she can accommodate only three more guests at her table. You gotta arrange ahead, like I did for you tonight. There's money left in the fund we started to bring you here. It's payin' the rent on that little house, but there's enough left to feed you. Besides," he added, leaning closer to Adam's shoulder, "the little lady needs the money. I should know—I'm the banker.''

As Pinter opened the front door of the boardinghouse, Adam noticed a small sign nailed to the siding an inch or two below eye level. The words *Almost Home* were painted across it in ornate script. He had missed it during his earlier visit.

Inside, Pinter led the way to the parlor. The shades were open, filling the room with afternoon sunshine. Two women were seated at opposite ends of the comfortably furnished room.

"Ah, the Cartland sisters are here already," Pinter said. "Ladies, have you met the new doctor?"

The women smiled and murmured their greetings. They were both in their thirties, Adam judged, and dressed rather elegantly, or at least more elegantly than Miss Sparks had been. He would have guessed they were sisters, for they had the same large nose.

Pinter took a few steps toward the window, putting him closer to one of the women. "This is Naomi," he said, "and yonder is Nedra."

Nedra's hair was an odd shade of yellow, while her sister's was…orange. Maybe unusual hair color ran in the family along with the nose.

"Come sit here, Doctor," said Nedra, indicating the space next to her on the velvet settee.

Adam tried to smile graciously as he crossed the room to join her.

"The ladies are planning to open a dress shop," Pinter said. "That will be such a welcome addition to the community, don't you think?"

The question rang with a certain amount of desperation. Catching Pinter's need for help with the conversation, Adam spoke up. "Where are you ladies from?"

"St. Louis," Nedra, the yellow-haired one, said. "Our father left us a small inheritance, and we decided we could make more of it out here than in the city."

"Our skills are needed here," declared Naomi, as if she saw their move in a very different light. "And

I don't just mean our sewing skills. These people are in desperate need of civilizing influences."

"The good doctor will help us with that," Nedra said, turning a radiant smile on Adam. "I understand you're from back east." She made it sound like a foreign country.

Before Adam could reply another guest entered the parlor. Pinter was quick to make the introduction. "Tim Martin, meet our new doctor, Adam Hart. Tim's a salesman. He makes the boarding-house his base whenever he's in the area."

Adam rose to shake the man's hand. He was middle-aged, his thin hair slightly graying.

"Good to meet you," Martin said. "I was out on a call this afternoon or I would have turned out with the rest to welcome you. Did the band play?"

Adam couldn't resist a smile at the memory of the band. "Yes, it was quite a welcome."

"Fine." He gave Adam a hearty slap on the back. "I love that band. Brings tears to my eyes every time I hear 'em." The lilt in his voice made Adam wonder if he meant tears of laughter.

"*It* could use some civilizing, if you ask me," Nedra said, tucking a strand of yellow hair in place. "I think they sound awful."

"It's their passion," Martin said, taking a seat and motioning for Adam to return to his. "I heard an interesting story today," he continued.

With the conversation in Martin's capable grasp, Adam found himself listening for sounds in the rest of the house, from the direction of the kitchen in particular. He was unaccountably eager for Miss Sparks to make her entrance, and not just because he was hungry.

Jane carried the last platter to the table. She had heard some of her boarders come down and knew they were gathering in the parlor. There would be seven at the table tonight. She had moved the extra chair to a corner to give the guests on one side of the table a little more room. George, she knew, would notice and take a seat there. Tim would probably take the other. She wondered which seat the doctor would take and why she pictured him at the head, directly across from her.

A quick inventory told her everything was in order but didn't banish the nervousness that had bothered her all afternoon. It was worry for Grams, she told herself for the twelfth time, not the prospect of eating dinner at the same table as the handsome young doctor.

The doctor unsettled her. The fact that his eyes and voice seemed kind and gentle didn't mean he was. She tried not to think about what he had suggested because it made her feel light-headed, but when she *did* think about it, she knew for certain that she had made the right choice. And Dr. Hart wasn't kind and gentle or he wouldn't have suggested such a thing.

But dinner was business. If George hadn't reserved a place for the doctor tonight, there'd be two empty chairs. Every meal meant that much more money toward the next house payment. Five more and the house would be hers. It would finally be a home.

Grams won't be here to see it.

The realization made tears threaten. She forced them aside and headed for the parlor. Five people sat visiting in the warm little room, but Dr. Adam Hart was the first one she saw. He had been watching the door instead of participating in the conversation. Their eyes locked and the intensity of his blue gaze captured hers. Darn, he was every bit as handsome as she remembered. One lock of sandy-brown hair fell across his forehead. She thought again that he seemed too young to be a doctor, though he was probably a year or two older than she was.

Tim Martin came to his feet, breaking the spell. "Ah, the lovely lady of the house has joined us."

In spite of her worries, Jane had to smile. She was far from lovely, especially now when she had had so little sleep. But Tim was a salesman. Complete honesty wasn't part of his nature. "May I escort you to dinner?" he asked, offering her his arm.

With a glance to make sure the rest of the guests were preparing to follow, she took his arm and walked with him to the dining room. He held her chair and she slipped into it. When the Cartland sisters were seated the men took their places.

"Mr. Bickford is late again," observed Nedra, giving Naomi a meaningful look. Naomi was silent.

The guests hadn't taken the chairs Jane had expected. Naomi, of course, had maneuvered her sister away from the center chair on the east side, ensuring the tardy Mr. Bickford would have to be seated next to her. But George had gone to the head of the table, and Tim had taken the chair beside him, leaving the doctor to sit at Jane's right.

George made the introductions.

"We've met," they said almost in unison. Now why should that completely fluster her? Her cheeks grew warm. Perhaps because she and the doctor had the attention of everyone around the table.

"I looked in on her grandmother this afternoon," the doctor explained.

"How is the old girl?" George asked, reaching for the bowl of potatoes that sat nearby and scooping up a mound for his plate. The others started dishes around as well, and Jane tried to force herself to relax.

"Not good," Dr. Hart answered.

Jane mentally crossed her fingers, hoping he would *not* describe what he had wanted to do. Fortunately, George didn't give him a chance to go into detail. "Too bad," he said, shaking his head. "We're all fond of Grams. Naomi, grab that butter dish there beside you and pass it on around."

The guests fell silent except for the clink of silver on china and a few murmured requests or thanks.

Jane would have been content for the meal to continue just that way.

"Miss Sparks," the young doctor began, "I was wondering if I could arrange to take all my meals here."

Why did that seem like a dangerous request? "I can't promise I'll always have a place for you," she heard herself say.

"Tomorrow morning?"

Jane pretended to think it over. Of course she had a place—two in fact. "Yes, you can come tomorrow morning. Beyond that, we'll have to wait and see."

He nodded. The table was quiet again for several minutes as her guests continued eating.

Tim was the next to speak. "You married, Adam?"

"Engaged," he said.

This created a minor stir around the table. Naomi expressed an interest in hearing about the fiancée, smirking a little at her sister's scowl. Perhaps Nedra had done a little maneuvering of her own. She sat directly across from the doctor.

"Her name's Doreena," Dr. Hart began. "She's very pretty, blond hair, kind of...well, I suppose *petite* is the right word."

"Little bitty thing, huh?" Tim asked, nudging Hart with his elbow.

The doctor grinned, which made him look even younger than he did already. "About this high," he said, touching his arm halfway between his elbow and his shoulder.

She was probably twelve, Jane thought uncharitably. Though she herself was an inch or two taller than the Cartlands, she had never felt overly tall. Never until now, anyway.

"She's accomplished on the piano," Adam added, obviously warming to the subject, to the neglect of the roasted chicken on his plate. "She paints a little and is a wonder when it comes to making all the arrangements for a party."

"Throws a good bash, does she?" Tim queried. "Sounds like quite a catch."

"Sounds like she's rich," Jane said. Just why she felt compelled to enter the conversation, she didn't know. Was she trying to offend a paying guest?

Instead of being offended, however, the doctor laughed and nodded. "That, too."

"Then she's definitely a catch," Tim said, joining in the laughter.

Jane forced herself to laugh, too, and wondered why she cared at all what the future Mrs. Hart was like.

The merriment died down rather abruptly, and Jane knew her final guest had arrived.

"Here you are," Naomi said in a voice that dripped with sweetness. "I was beginning to worry about you."

"The novel, you know. The term will start soon and there will be no time to work on it."

"This is Lawrence Bickford, our schoolmaster," George said. "Have you met Dr. Hart?"

Bickford shook his head as he took his seat. "I understand you're from Philadelphia."

"Dr. Hart was telling us about his fiancée," Naomi said as she made sure all the bowls and platters were passed to the late arrival. Jane doubted if he noticed her efforts.

"Don't get discouraged, lad," Bickford said as he filled his plate. "Your year in the wilds will fly by and you'll be together again."

"Actually, I'm hoping she'll join me in a few months," Adam said. "I want to make a home here."

Jane tried to work up some irritation toward the prospect of a piano-playing, party-planning neighbor. Instead she felt an odd pain at the thought of seeing the perfect Doreena at Adam's side.

"A wedding," Naomi cooed. "Isn't that romantic?" She asked the question of the table at large, but her eyes had turned to the schoolmaster. He made no response.

Jane might have enjoyed Naomi's attempts to gain Mr. Bickford's attention if she weren't feeling somehow ill at ease. Because of her grandmother, she told herself, though to be honest she had nearly forgotten the poor woman for a few minutes. Concentration seemed to be a casualty of sleepless nights.

"Please, excuse me," she said, coming to her

feet. "I must check on Grams. Enjoy your dinner and stay as long as you like." Being careful that her glance never met the doctor's, she left the room. She was afraid his eyes would be condemning. He knew she had chosen to let Grams die.

Grams was sleeping, but Jane sat down beside her anyway, dampening the cloth and returning it to her forehead. She lifted one of Grams's hands, thinking how hot and brittle it felt. The old woman's pulse seemed to flutter beneath her fingers.

"I shouldn't have even sat down with them," Jane whispered. "I should have stayed with you."

Voices drifted in from the other room, George's primarily. She didn't try to understand what was being said. She wanted to be alone with Grams.

"Remember when we first came here, Grams?" she asked softly. "I wanted to go home. You said, 'This can be home, Janie. Anywhere someone loves you is home.'"

Jane felt her eyes burn. She hadn't come in here to cry. But she had fought the tears so often the last few days there was no strength left to fight them. "Don't go, Grams," she whispered, lowering her face to her hands. "Don't go."

Chapter Two

Adam lost interest in dinner shortly after Jane left. He would have excused himself as well, but the Cartland sisters were extremely interested in his wedding plans, which were few, and his plans for decorating the house, which were even fewer.

Tim Martin began describing a wedding he had attended in another part of the state, and Adam struck on a plan. He could almost convince himself he was being professional.

"Friends," he said when Martin gave him an opening, "I believe I'll check on Miss Sparks's grandmother, then call it a night."

"Why, that's so kind of you," Nedra said.

He gave her a polite smile as he rose. She had been batting her eyes at him all through dinner, and he didn't want to encourage her. The others, except for Mr. Bickford, wished him good-night as he left the dining room.

The kitchen bore the evidence of the huge meal

Jane had recently prepared. Adam wondered if her entire store of pots and pans had been called into service. Still, the room seemed clean in spite of it, a trick of organization, perhaps.

He moved cautiously toward the little bedroom. He didn't want to startle Jane, yet he didn't want to disturb the sick grandmother by calling out to them. At the doorway he paused. Jane sat beside the bed, her face in her hands. She was crying softly. He could hear the grandmother's labored breathing above the quiet sobs.

He felt like an intruder, but he couldn't make himself leave. He moved to the far side of the bed and lifted Grams's bony hand, feeling for the pulse. It was faint and rapid. He gently returned the hand to its place on the sheet.

He should leave. There was nothing he could do for the old lady. Nothing he could do for the granddaughter, either, he told himself. Wrapping her in his arms and letting her cry on his shoulder didn't seem very professional. Besides, judging by the cool glances she had given him at dinner, she wouldn't be disposed to accept.

He rested his hand gently on the cloth that lay across the woman's forehead. It was cool and damp. Even in the state she was in, Jane hadn't neglected this small service.

She would be embarrassed if she looked up and found him watching her, Adam knew. He ordered his legs to take him out of the room, but found himself stopping beside Miss Sparks instead. His hand was drawn to the narrow, slumped shoulder.

At the moment of contact her head jerked upright. "Doctor. I didn't hear you come in." She brushed frantically at her tear-streaked face.

Adam crouched down beside her. "I didn't mean to startle you."

"Is she...?"

"Not much change from this afternoon. Are you all right?" He wanted her to say no, to ask him to stay with her.

"Of course." She sniffed once. "Did somebody need something?"

He shook his head. It seemed to him she was the only one who needed anything, and he didn't know how to give it. "Let me ask the folks out there to clean up for you."

"Oh, you can't do that," she said, rising to her feet. "They're paying guests."

Adam straightened slowly. "They're also your friends."

"No, please. I can do it. I can check on Grams every few minutes."

"Then let me stay and help."

"Don't be silly. I'm used to doing it, really."

She was all but shooing him out of the room. He took the hint, but at the door he turned. "There might still be time, you know. We should do everything we can to save her."

Jane shook her head. "No. She's dying. But I couldn't see her in pain any longer."

Adam nodded. It was what he expected. Back in the kitchen, he could hear voices from the dining room. He had already told the others good-night, and, not wanting to see Nedra again quite so soon, he left through the back door.

Miss Sparks's backyard contained a tidy garden and shed, clotheslines and a small chicken house and pen, making his own yard seem barren. The sun was just sinking below the horizon as he reached his back door. His first day here hadn't turned out to be quite what he expected. His little house seemed too quiet and lonely as he went up the stairs to his bedroom.

He lit a lamp and lifted a book from the pile he had left against a wall. Shelves here and in the examining room were a top priority. He would look into hiring a carpenter tomorrow.

He removed his shoes, coat and tie and worked the collar buttons loose. He settled onto the bed, his back against the headboard. The book lay unopened on his lap as he listened to voices next door. The Cartland sisters were on the porch. There were men's voices as well, bidding one another good-night.

After a brief silence, a feminine voice carried to his room. "It's a lovely night, isn't it, Mr. Bickford?"

A gruff, unintelligible response followed.

"I was hoping you'd join us on the swing for a while."

Adam heard a grumbled reply, followed by the muffled slam of a door.

"Really, Naomi, how can you stand that man?"

"He's cultured and educated," her sister hissed. "I can smooth out the rough edges once we're married. That's what women have always done."

"Rough edges? The man's a self-absorbed lout."

Naomi didn't disagree, and Adam felt a grin tug at his lips. If Mr. Bickford's window was open the self-absorbed lout could probably hear this conversation, too.

"At least I'm not throwing myself at someone half my age." That must have been Naomi.

"The doctor isn't half my age. Five years younger, perhaps."

"Try ten."

"He's cultured and educated, too."

"With a beautiful fiancée."

"Who isn't here. And until she is, he can only compare me to the country milkmaids and slum trash like Jane."

"And me, of course."

"You won't try to ruin this for me, will you?"

"Why shouldn't I try? *You* can have Mr. Bickford."

Adam realized he had nearly stopped breathing. It was one thing to listen to their conversation about Mr. Bickford and quite another to be the topic himself. It wasn't so much learning that Nedra was interested in him that bothered him; he had figured that out at dinner. It was the calculating way they were discussing him.

And Jane. Did they look down on her because of humble beginnings? Letting them know his own roots should discourage them quickly enough. He would try to work it into the conversation at breakfast if he weren't certain Doreena would prefer it not be known.

He realized he didn't simply want to discourage the sisters, he wanted to defend Jane. That struck him as odd because he hardly knew her, apart from the fact that she was a great cook. She was going through a rough time, and while he disagreed with her decision about her grandmother, he felt certain it was for reasons that she, at least, found compelling. The notion that she was allowing Grams to die so the boardinghouse would be hers, or the possibility that she was simply tired of caring for the old woman, had crossed his mind and been dismissed.

Adam had to respect Jane's wishes. In disagreeing with his authority, she had shown herself to be a strong woman. He smiled at his own thoughts. Her disagreement would be more impressive if he was an older, more respected physician. He was making excuses for her and she didn't need that.

He laid the book aside and moved to the window. The boardinghouse was in shadows now, but he was certain no one remained on the porch.

What did Jane need?

Not his help. Not even his company.

Grams might linger for a day or two, but he doubted it. She would probably die tonight. In spite of the boarders in the rooms upstairs, Jane would be alone. And Adam couldn't think of any way to ease her sorrow or his own guilt.

Jane sat in the straight-backed chair beside Grams's bed and held a hot, fragile hand gently in her own. She had slept in the chair the past two nights, but tonight sleep wouldn't come. It had taken until nearly midnight to clean up the kitchen and dining room. She had hated to leave her grandmother even for a few minutes, afraid she would die alone.

Now, as the clock ticked toward three o'clock, she thought of all the things she wanted to tell her grandmother. She prayed that Grams would wake up one more time so Jane could tell her how much she loved her. She would tell her how grateful she was for all the things Grams had taught her. She would…

The breathing stopped abruptly. Just like that. Jane stared at the beloved face. "Grams?"

The hand she held was still hot, but the pulse she'd felt a moment before had stilled. Grams was gone.

Jane had thought she was prepared for this but she found herself shaking. Unshed tears burned behind her eyes and formed a lump in her throat. She would have to face a future without Grams.

"I won't give up," she whispered. "I won't lose the boardinghouse. I'll work hard and make you proud, Grams."

Adam arrived for breakfast at the appointed hour and found the parlor deserted. George stepped into the hall and motioned him toward the dining room. "The old lady died last night," he said softly. "Such a shame. Jane's gone to make the arrangements and has asked the Cartlands to fix breakfast. We're trying to set the table."

Tim Martin was arranging plates and coffee cups, while Lawrence Bickford lounged against the sideboard. "What do you think?" Martin asked.

"Does it matter?" Adam replied. "As long as we've got what we need to eat with."

"Dr. Hart, I'm surprised at you!" One of the Cartlands, the one with orange hair, had come in from the kitchen with a plate of biscuits. *O* for orange; it was Naomi. She gave him what could only be described as an indulgent smile. "The forks go on the left and the knives on the right," she instructed Martin sternly before flouncing back into the kitchen.

"You've been overruled," Martin said softly. He went to work switching the flatware on his side of the table, and Adam stepped up to take care of the other.

"How is Miss Sparks holding up?" he asked.

"Haven't seen her," Martin answered. "Have you, George?"

"Early this morning. She was her usual efficient self. She said her grandmother just slipped away in her sleep. It was a mercy, really. Ah, here comes breakfast."

The Cartland sisters paraded in, one with a platter of scrambled eggs and the other with sliced ham. Nedra spoke as she approached the table. "George, would you get the coffee? I swear that pot is just too heavy for either of us to be carrying around."

George moved quickly to do her bidding.

When Naomi approached a chair near where he stood, Adam automatically stepped forward to hold it for her. Her flirtatious smile made him curse his ingrained manners.

Naomi was in Jane's place, Adam to her right and Nedra to her left. George filled the coffee cups, and, when he was seated, the Cartlands started the platters around the table.

"Cooking for this many people is quite an experience," Naomi commented.

The eggs were so rubbery Adam was sure he saw them bounce when he dropped them on his plate.

"So many things to watch at once," her sister concurred. "Why, I swear it would tax less intelligent women."

Adam heard a biscuit actually clink against George's plate.

"Jane makes it look so easy," Martin commented.

Naomi tossed her head as if the comment was inconsequential. "I suppose if one has no other skills, cooking for large groups of people would at least be something."

Her sister nodded. "But we thought it was our duty to be of help to poor Jane."

The men politely murmured their understanding and thankfulness. All of the women's comments had been directed toward Adam, and they watched his every move. He took a sip of coffee and put the cup down quickly, hoping they hadn't seen his grimace, then hoping they had. They had used an egg to settle the grounds, but the coffee had been allowed to boil again afterward, leaving it tasting more like eggs than the eggs on his plate.

Adam tried to eat a little of the poorly prepared food, telling himself that it was the nutrition that counted. A glance around the table told him the other men were doing the same.

"There might be something to be said for practice," Naomi commented.

Murmurs of agreement echoed around the table.

"Tell me, Adam," Nedra began. "I *can* call you Adam, *can't* I?" She fluttered her heavily blackened eyelashes.

"Of course." If he took small enough bites of the biscuit and chewed it long enough his stomach

ought to be able to digest it, he reasoned. It couldn't
be any worse than the hardtack soldiers ate.

"So tell me, Adam." She actually giggled.
"What do you think of our little town so far?"

Adam swallowed, then took a sip of the coffee-
and-egg brew to be sure it went down. "Well," he
said, "the people are certainly friendly."

"Of course they are," Naomi said, obviously trying to draw his attention away from Nedra. "You
should let me show you around."

"Wouldn't that be fun?" Nedra said. "We could
do it anytime."

Naomi's eyes shot venom at her sister, but Nedra
didn't notice; she was too intent on Adam.

Adam thought again of mentioning his humble
beginnings, but somehow, initiating any conversation with either of these women seemed risky. He
glanced at Mr. Bickford and found him eating as if
he were the only one present. Perhaps experience
had taught him to keep his thoughts to himself.

"Well, I'm off to the bank," George said, rising
from the table. "Can I get anyone more coffee before I go?" Adam wasn't surprised that there were
no takers.

With the ice broken, the rest found it easy to leave
as well. Adam was back in his empty little house in
no time. After the initial elation of being away from
the Cartland sisters came the more sobering realization that, until he had a patient, he didn't have
much to do. He wished again that Doreena had con-

sented to come with him. He would at least have company while he waited.

He slouched in one of the chairs in his front room and gazed at his surroundings. He wanted to hire a carpenter to build the shelves. And he ought to lay in some food in case the Cartlands cooked again.

He laughed out loud. "That was the worst meal I've ever eaten," he said softly. If nothing else, it had prepared him for Doreena's inexperience. She couldn't possibly do worse.

It wouldn't do him any good to sit and think about Doreena all day. He would put a note on his door and run his errands. The task was done almost as quickly as the decision was made, and in a moment he was bounding down the steps.

He stopped and inhaled deeply. The air smelled fresher than what he was used to, clean and sweet with just a touch of wood smoke. He hadn't noticed yesterday, in the confusion of the welcoming committee and the fear for his first patient.

His first patient. He had to put her and her granddaughter out of his mind. He headed down the dirt street, determined to enjoy his first full day in the West, which was proving to be less wild than the novels had described. It was just as well, he supposed. He didn't really want to be treating gunshot wounds on steely eyed gunmen.

It was the independence and the opportunities he had come for, a chance to live free from the constraints of a society that didn't quite include him, yet wanted to govern his every move. This pretty little town was the perfect place for him.

Clyde's business district started only a block and a half from his house—and ended three blocks beyond that, where a bridge crossed a little creek. A hard-packed path served as a sidewalk. A few small trees had been planted to separate the path from the street a few feet away.

Adam walked the entire length of Washington Street, then crossed it and started back. He discovered several grocery stores, some in unlikely combination with other things like shoes or livestock feed. One was combined with a drugstore, and Adam stepped inside.

After arranging with Mr. McIntosh to supply him with medicine once his own supply ran low, he purchased a few canned goods and staples, mindful of the fact that he would have to carry them home.

"Is there a carpenter in town?" he asked as McIntosh tallied his purchases.

"Yep," he said. "J. H. Huff down the street. He can build about anything you can imagine."

Adam billed the groceries to his account at the bank and, with the gunnysack the grocer had provided filled with survival food, he crossed the street.

Adam found the carpenter's shop by the smell of sawdust. A carpenter was hard at work smoothing the surface of a long pine board. Something about the way several more pieces of wood were laid out on the floor amid the shavings caught Adam's attention. He set his sack on the floor and watched the man work for a minute, putting off calling attention to himself until he had solved the puzzle.

It hit him all at once. It was to be a coffin, probably for Adam's first patient. He should feel regret or even irritation at the granddaughter for not allowing him to try to save her. Instead all he felt was deep sympathy for Jane.

Huff broke into his thoughts. "Howdy, sonny. What can I do you for?"

Adam was momentarily startled by the odd syntax. "I wondered if you could build some shelves for me?"

"Start this afternoon. You want wall or free?"

That, too, took a second to decipher. "Wall, I mean fastened to the wall."

"Ya live…?" The man was still holding the plane as if he intended to apply it to the wood again in a second. Perhaps his cryptic speech was intended to save time.

"Little place just past the boardinghouse."

Huff nodded, pointing a corner of the plane toward him for an instant. "New doctor."

Adam nodded.

"Afternoon." He returned to his work.

It was only midmorning, so Adam took that as a reminder rather than a salutation. He hoisted the gunnysack over his shoulder, leaving the rasp of the plane behind him.

On his way home he met a few townspeople who

nodded or murmured greetings, but nobody seemed interested in stopping to talk. What, he wondered, was he going to do with himself the rest of the morning?

As he passed the boardinghouse he hit on an idea. He could visit Jane. He could offer his condolences and, if she wasn't too distraught, he could ask about a seat at the table for dinner. He expected to be starving by then. Why that particular errand could lighten his steps, he wasn't sure. Boredom, probably.

He left his sack inside his front door, edited his sign to read Next Door instead of In Town, and hurried to the boardinghouse. Inside, he straightened his collar and tie and ran his fingers through his hair. That too seemed an odd reaction, but he passed it off as wanting to look respectable considering the errand.

The house was quiet. A house of mourning, he reminded himself. He walked softly to the dining room and stopped in surprise. The table was exactly as he had left it an hour or more before. Dirty plates, half-full coffee cups, the uneaten ham, all lay drying on the table.

He had assumed the Cartlands would clean up. Obviously they had assumed otherwise. They had left it for Jane. He guessed that Jane had been up all night, out early making arrangements for a funeral and was now trying to get a little rest. This was not the sight that should greet her when she awoke.

Adam shrugged out of his suit coat and swung it over the back of a chair. He had pulled kitchen duty for larger groups than this. He expertly stacked plates and saucers and headed for the kitchen.

And met his second surprise. The mess in the kitchen defied imagination. The Cartlands hadn't replaced a single lid on any of the canisters and tins they had opened, let alone started a pan to soak. There was even a broken egg lying on the floor just where it had been dropped. With a sigh he attacked the mess, reminding himself that he had nothing else to do.

An hour later the kitchen looked like Jane's again. He had found where most things belonged or at least made a guess and left the rest stacked on the now-clean table. He rolled down his sleeves and looked around, satisfied with his work. He gathered the collar and buttons and his tie from the chair where he had discarded them earlier, and returned to the dining room.

Clean dishes now filled the glass-fronted cabinet, and the hardwood table shone from the oil and lemon polish he had found. He had even swept the floor. There was nothing left to do, which should make him happy. Cleaning was not his favorite activity.

But he didn't want to go back to his empty house. He had been imagining Doreena in the boardinghouse kitchen, and he had trouble picturing her in the smaller house.

Well, part of the time he had imagined Doreena. The rest of the time he had pictured Jane finding a spot on one of her dishes. Or worse, finding him in her kitchen up to his elbows in dishwater, with sweat plastering his hair to his forehead. Collarless with his shirt open and his coat off. She was liable to be scandalized. Or embarrassed. Neither was his intent.

He slipped the collar and tie into a pocket of his coat and slung it over his shoulder just as he heard a door close down the hall. Light, feminine footsteps approached the dining room. He was about to confront either Jane or one of the Cartland sisters. He considered making a run for the back door, but ran his fingers through his damp hair instead.

Jane entered the room, her purposeful steps faltering when she saw him.

"I seem to make a habit of startling you," he said.

"What are you doing here?"

"Ah...." He debated telling her.

"Is it getting hot out?" she asked.

"Warm," he said. "I came to offer my condolences."

"Thanks." She nodded and turned away, going through the kitchen door. Adam sighed to himself. She really didn't like him. And, he told himself firmly, it really didn't matter.

He followed her into the kitchen. "Perhaps this

isn't a good time,'' he said to her back as she lifted a bowl off a cupboard shelf, "but I was wondering if there would be room for me at dinner.''

"Sorry,'' she said, continuing her work. "The pastor and his wife are coming to dinner, and that fills the table, I'm afraid.''

Adam thought of several other things he might say, but they all seemed trite in the face of her obvious grief. He was turning to go when the door opened and Tim Martin entered.

"I'm off to catch the train,'' the salesman said.

The glance Jane threw in Adam's direction before she turned to her boarder held a combination of irritation and guilt. She had known Martin was leaving but had denied his request for dinner anyway.

"Have a safe trip, Tim,'' she said pleasantly. "Can I expect you back in a couple of months?''

"Of course, and I'll recommend you to everyone I see that's headed your way. Sorry about your grandmother, dear. It was nice meeting you, Doctor.''

Martin shook hands with Adam, turned and kissed Jane's cheek, then left them alone again.

Adam watched Jane avoid his eyes. Finally she muttered, "I forgot he was leaving today.''

Adam nodded, not believing her at all.

"Dinner will be the same time as last night.'' She turned back to her work.

"Miss Sparks, if you don't want me to eat here, I can—''

"No," she said quickly, facing him. "Please, I don't want an empty chair if I can help it."

He grinned at her. "That's wonderfully flattering."

"I'm not good at flattery."

She turned away, and he watched her stiff shoulders for a moment, wondering why he didn't just leave. "We missed you this morning," he said finally.

She shrugged.

"I mean, we *really* missed you this morning."

She faced him, her eyes narrowed in question. He quirked a smile at her. "I'm looking forward to dinner."

Jane watched him walk out of the room and listened for the front door to close. She tried to brush the image of that little-boy grin out of her mind. What exactly had he meant by missing her at breakfast? She might have thought he was suggesting the meal had been inadequate, but she knew better. Nedra had already told her it had been fine.

Jane also knew better than to think it was her company he had missed. She had been nothing but rude to him since she'd met him. And even if she had been sweet and gracious, he had Doreena.

She set the flour-coated teacup aside and sank into the chair. She had come in with every intention of baking pies for dinner. She had gotten as far as measuring two cups of flour. Or was it three? She would have to pour it back and start again.

Why did Dr. Adam Hart get her so rattled?

She wanted to laugh at herself. Besides the fact that his face was so handsome he made her knees weak and his body was the very model of masculine health? Maybe because he thought she had let her grandmother die.

She would like to tell him all her reasons, and she would, if she felt more certain of them. Right now she didn't. Right now she thought he was right—she should have let him try anything to save Grams.

And that was what bothered her about Dr. Hart. She associated him with the pain and the loss and the guilt. And she always would.

She forced herself back to her feet and thoughts of Dr. Hart out of her mind. She had dinner to prepare. And it would be one of her best. She would make up for missing breakfast. She poured the flour back into the canister and measured out six cups. Salt, then lard followed. She reached for her pastry cutter in its usual place, but it wasn't there. She tried two other drawers before she found it. Evidently the Cartlands had used it for the biscuits and had forgotten where it went. The minor irritation was easily forgotten.

Chapter Three

They buried Grams the next morning.

As he stood at the chilly cemetery with the others, Adam found himself watching Jane. She seemed in complete control but the tight jaw and rigid spine testified to what it cost her. Even from where he stood he could see the dark shadows under her eyes.

Following the service, everyone went to the boardinghouse. Adam was sure the entire town and half the countryside were crowded into Jane's parlor and dining room. He found a place against a wall of the parlor and watched the proceedings with interest. It seemed more like a party than a funeral except that voices were kept appropriately subdued.

Three gentlemen nearby introduced themselves. "Gonna miss that old gal," one said.

"Shame somebody so lively should come down with dropsy," commented a second.

"It was pneumonia," Adam said.

The man nodded. "Once she was down in bed, I

figured that'd happen. Her granddaughter took her to Kansas City a month or so ago. Old lady was against it. Waste of money. But she was slowing down and her feet were always swollen, and the girl needed to know why.''

"Don't dropsy mean a bad heart?" asked another. "Such a shame. The pneumonia was really a blessing."

The three men left in search of food, leaving Adam to stare after them. Jane hadn't mentioned a heart condition, though she had said something about it being hopeless. He should have questioned her.

But the pneumonia had been so obvious he hadn't considered other illnesses at all. What kind of a doctor would make a mistake like that? A young one, he supposed. Still, it bothered him. A lot. He felt he owed Jane an apology for any additional anguish he might have caused her.

He had some thought of seeking her out for that purpose when a middle-aged woman stepped up beside him. "You must be the new doctor."

"That's right. Adam Hart." He extended his hand.

"I'm Rose Finley," she said, taking the hand and not letting it go. "I saw you get off the train, but you're even better looking up close."

Adam laughed self-consciously. "That's kind of you," he said, finally extricating his hand.

"But you're so young," she added.

His own thoughts exactly. "Yes, ma'am. Only time's going to cure that."

"Oh, and clever, too. Is your wife here?"

"I'm not married."

"You poor thing," she said. She looked anything but sympathetic.

"Would you excuse me?" He made his way around her and added over his shoulder, "It was nice meeting you, Mrs. Finley."

There was a steady flow of people in and out of the parlor, some carrying plates of food, others holding coffee cups. The hall and the dining room were nearly as crowded. The chairs that normally circled the table had been placed against the wall, along with at least a dozen others. The table was spread with the largest assortment of food Adam had ever seen in one place.

He searched the room for Jane and found her lifting a stack of plates out of the china cupboard. She set the plates on a corner of the table. Before Adam could make his way toward her, she turned and spoke to a woman who had approached her carrying a silver coffee server.

He watched Jane take it and thank the woman, then turn toward the kitchen. Evidently the woman had been reporting that the server was empty. Jane had gone to the kitchen to fill it from the pot that was too heavy for the Cartland sisters to lift.

George Pinter hampered Adam's progress toward

the kitchen. "Quite a spread, huh?" the little man asked with a smile.

"I hope she didn't cook all of this."

"You mean Jane? No, most of the women here brought something. Might as well grab a plate and dig in."

Adam cast another look toward the open kitchen door before he followed Pinter to the table. "Is this what all funerals are like out here?" he asked.

"Somewhat. But everybody was fond of Grams. It's a tragedy." He shook his head and repeated, "A real tragedy."

Adam expected him to add in the next breath that it was a blessing.

Pinter found two empty chairs and motioned for Adam to join him. From across the room, Adam watched Jane pour coffee into outstretched cups, accept dirty dishes and clean up one or two minor spills. "Isn't she supposed to be the primary mourner here?" he asked.

"Jane? I suppose. But she probably wouldn't accept help if anyone offered."

"*Has* anyone offered?"

George shrugged. "Did you try this apple strudel? I'll bet anything it's Jane's."

Adam shook his head. "Save this seat." With a purposeful stride, his dirty plate held out in front of him, he made it to the kitchen without being stopped for more than a greeting. He set his plate on the table and blocked Jane's way as she headed out with another server of coffee.

"Go sit down," he said.

"What? People are waiting for more coffee."

"They can get their own coffee." At her shocked expression he put his hand next to hers on the silver handle. "Or you can let me pour it. Fill a plate and go sit by Mr. Pinter."

She made no move to relinquish the server and Adam wondered what was going through her mind. "This is crazy, you know," he said softly. "Your grandmother dies and you're expected to throw a party for the whole town? We should all be waiting on you."

She almost smiled, but her grip on the coffee server tightened. "That's a little hard to picture. Look, Doctor, I know you mean well, but this is what I do."

Adam eased his hand away, and she brushed past him. He made his way slowly back to his chair.

"What was that about?" Pinter asked as Adam sat down.

"I offered to help. You were right."

Pinter laughed and the sound grated against Adam's ears, as had all the other laughter he had heard this morning. "Don't take it so hard, son. Your mama'd be proud you offered."

Adam swallowed laughter of his own. He knew some woman had given birth to him, but it had been years since he had thought about it. The notion that she might have a moment of pride on his account seemed ludicrous. "That wasn't the point," he muttered.

A few minutes later the first of the guests decided to leave. Adam kept his seat and watched them approach Jane. A few remembered to offer their condolences along with their thanks for the lunch. Scattered dishes on the table left with their owners. The pace of the departures increased until he was the only one remaining.

Jane walked slowly back to the dining room after seeing the last of the guests out. She knew Dr. Hart was still sitting in there. She would have noticed if he had left with the rest. It was too much to hope that he had gone out the back door while she wasn't looking.

No, she was right. There he was. At least he had the manners to come to his feet when she entered the room. Could that possibly mean he was finally ready to leave?

That hope died with his words. "You look exhausted."

"Is that your medical opinion?" She decided to tackle the table first, starting with the empty platters.

"Yeah, but it's free."

"That's about what it's worth." She didn't want to find the doctor amusing. She didn't want to be attracted to a man engaged to a beautiful, wealthy woman. If he would just go away she wouldn't have to think about him—at least not as much. "Don't you have patients to see?"

"Apparently not. This may be the healthiest town in the country." He was using a large empty platter as a tray and filling it with cups that were lying around the room.

She watched him a moment, marveling at his efficient movements. Actually, marveling at more than that until she remembered she wanted to send him away. "How will you know if you have patients if you aren't home when they come?"

"There's a note on the door that says I'm here." He carried the platter of dishes into her kitchen.

She quickly followed him. "Are you mad at me for not letting you pour coffee? Is that why you're hanging around?"

"No." His back was to her and it took her a moment to tear her eyes away from the wide expanse of shoulders and notice what he was doing. He pumped water into her dishpan and placed it on her stove. Flicking a drop of water on his finger he tested the temperature of the stovetop.

When he started to remove his suit coat, she found her voice. "What are you doing?"

He paused for only an instant, then the coat came off, reminding her of the other time she had seen him in his shirtsleeves. A suspicion tickled the back of her mind but he spoke, distracting her. "I was going to wash, but I could dry if you'd rather."

"Do I look so bad that you think I need help?"

He was removing his tie, and it demanded her full attention. Long, clever fingers worked a collar button loose. Then another. In a moment the collar and tie were stuffed into a pocket of the coat he had kept over his arm, and his throat was exposed.

"I owe you an apology," he said, and she found herself reaching for the coat as he handed it to her. He rolled up his sleeves as he talked. "I was wrong about your grandmother."

Jane blinked. "Apparently not."

"I mean, I was right about the pneumonia. But I didn't know about the dropsy."

"I told you…" She watched him shake his head and realized that she hadn't. "I'm sorry."

"No, it was my fault. I should have asked more questions."

How many men could admit their mistakes so easily, or were willing to accept blame that was partially hers? How many men had eyes that shade of blue?

Jane shook her head. Dr. Hart was a distraction she didn't need. "You're forgiven," she said, "and you don't have to help with the dishes to make amends."

He grinned at that, that charming little-boy grin that made her want to smile. "Let me be honest," he said, as if he were about to share a secret. "I've never lived alone before. In fact, I don't think I've ever *been* alone before. That house gives me the creeps."

He turned away, opened a cabinet door and withdrew a tray. "I bet there are dishes in the parlor."

Jane followed him with slow steps, stunned by the turn of events. His steps, on the other hand, were purposeful, and he outdistanced her in a moment. She stood in her messy dining room, staring at the empty doorway to the hall.

And caressing Dr. Hart's suit coat. As soon as she realized what she was doing, she put it over the back of a chair. He was determined to stay and help her clean up. It was foolish to argue about it. First, because she didn't think he would give in, and second, because she *was* exhausted.

She would concentrate on his "secret" and put her grandmother's death out of her mind for a little while. She was still standing two steps inside the dining room when he returned with the tray of dishes.

"You need a dog," she said as she followed him into the kitchen. He turned and grinned at her. He looked exactly like a little boy who had just been offered a puppy. "How old are you?" she asked.

He laughed. It was a very pleasant laugh, and she decided she needed that even more than she needed his help.

He found a place for the tray and turned back to her. "Think of how much trouble I'd be in if I asked you that."

"All right. I'll assume you're older than you look,

and you can assume I'm younger than I look. How's that?"

"You really think I look so young?"

His grin was the kind that took over his whole face. It was incredibly charming. And incredibly dangerous. "Let me wash," she said. "You can dry if you want to."

"You're avoiding the question, but I suppose that's an answer. Maybe that's why I don't have any patients. They think I'm too young."

She moved the pan of warmed water to the counter, glad that she could turn her back on him. She had a tendency to want to gaze at him and not get her work done. "You don't have any patients yet because folks aren't used to going for help. They tend to take care of themselves."

Until they're desperate, she would have added, but she didn't want any reminder of his visits to Grams. It was there, of course, always between them, but unspoken was preferable to spoken.

He was silent for a few minutes, giving her a chance to get some glasses washed in peace. "In other words," he said, opening the drawer that contained her tea towels, "I can expect to see only severe cases at first."

There it was, too close to spoken. She swallowed a lump in her throat. "Yes," she managed to answer.

She was grateful that he said no more about it. She washed and he dried, carrying trays full of her dishes to the cabinet in the dining room and bringing back more dirty dishes with each trip. "That's the last in there," he said finally. "Why don't you do something with the food while I clean up the table?"

He found the furniture polish and was gone before she could agree or disagree. But why would she have disagreed? They were making their way through the mess much more quickly than she could have on her own. And he was surprisingly efficient help.

Oddly enough, she had wanted to disagree. It was her boardinghouse, and she prided herself on being self-sufficient. She hated to admit she needed help. She hated even more to admit she enjoyed his company. She had no time for a man in her life, even if she wanted one, which she most certainly did not. Besides, he had Doreena.

He returned to the kitchen, put the polish away and grabbed a fresh tea towel. "So what happens if I get a dog and he bothers the neighbors?"

His eager tone made her laugh out loud, surprising herself. "Since I'm your only close neighbor, I suppose that would be me. Let's see." She was washing the large platters now. She could hear the gentle clatter as he carefully stacked them on the table.

"As a matter of fact, your dog could cause me a lot of trouble. He could pull my laundry off the line, chew up my favorite tablecloth, dig up my flowers, accost my guests—"

"No," he interrupted. "No accosting. I'd train him better than that."

"So what about my flowers and my clothes?"

"Puppies are puppies." There was that grin again, so infectious she couldn't help smiling.

"And my favorite tablecloth?"

"I'd buy you a new one. If I ever get any patients." She watched him slowly turn serious. "Probably not a good idea," he said.

"I was teasing, Adam." She had a sudden notion that perhaps he had never had a chance to be a little boy. She would bet his childhood hadn't included a puppy.

"How's this?" she suggested. "If you treat a farmer or his family and he offers you a pig as payment, ask if he's got any puppies instead."

Adam looked stunned. "Offers a pig as payment? You are joking, aren't you?"

She laughed and turned back to the dishes.

"Pigs," he muttered. He lifted the stack of platters and, just before he took it to the dining room, added, "If I get paid with a pig, I'm paying for my dinners with it."

Jane fought the urge to giggle. The situation was too bizarre. Here she was laughing with a man whom she swore she didn't like, letting him help her with dishes, of all things. Well, she *did* like him; she couldn't help that. He would be as impossible to dislike as that puppy they were talking about.

She heard voices in the dining room and realized

the clatter of dishes had kept her from hearing the front door. Grabbing a towel to dry her hands, she went out to investigate.

"He's in the wagon," a woman was saying.

"You go make sure he doesn't move," Adam told her. "I'll be right out."

The woman, a farm wife Jane knew only vaguely, hurried to do as Adam said.

Adam turned to her, tossing the tea towel over her shoulder. "Sorry I can't help you finish."

Jane shook her head, but he had already turned away. A need to watch him with a patient other than Grams sent her after him. She stood on her porch as he leaned over the wagon. The sideboards hid the patient from Jane's view, but a small foot extending out the back made her realize it was the woman's son, not husband that she had brought to town.

Adam spoke softly, the encouraging tones reaching Jane's ears if not the words. The woman nodded and took his place at the back of the wagon while he ran into his house. Jane walked down her steps and joined the woman.

"What happened, Mrs. Tallon?" she asked, the name coming to her when she saw the six-year-old boy's face. "How did Billy get hurt?"

"Oh, Miss Sparks," the woman said, reaching out to her. "He fell trying to build a tree house. I told him to wait 'til his father could help him."

"Aunt Jane!" the boy cried. His mother moved

quickly to keep him still. "Doc says my leg's busted."

"Well, don't sound so proud," his mother scolded.

"It hurt a lot at first," Billy confided. "But now it don't hurt less'en I move it."

Adam joined them with splints and his medical bag. Jane stepped out of his way but watched over his shoulder as he cut the boy's trouser leg from the ankle.

"So what do you think, Doc?" she asked. "Can little boys with broken legs still eat cookies?"

Even where she stood she could see Adam grin at Billy. "I don't know. A diet of spinach and beets is what I usually recommend."

Billy looked dismayed for a moment, then grinned back. "You're just funnin' me."

Jane took Mrs. Tallon's hand. "When the doctor gets through tying him back together, bring him over for a cookie before you head home."

"That's so sweet of you," the woman said, "but we can't. I'll need to get home and start dinner. I'll have Billy's chores to do now, too."

"Of course. Say, I have all kinds of food left from the funeral dinner. I'd be pleased if you'd take it home to your husband and boys."

"Funeral dinner? Your grandmother?" Mrs. Tallon put her arm around Jane's shoulder. "I'm sorry, Miss Sparks. I hadn't heard."

"I understand," Jane said quickly, not wanting to

dwell on the funeral. "Now that dinner's taken care of, you have time to bring Billy by for a cookie. I'll go box up the food."

Jane hurried back to her kitchen, uncertain why she had a sudden need to get away. The mention of the funeral, probably. She had managed to forget about it for a while. She had needed something like this to bring her back to her senses. She was starting to have too much fun teasing Dr. Adam Hart.

Grams was barely underground, and Jane was already forgetting her advice. *Don't trust men with anything but business. Don't depend on them, and don't let them know your weaknesses.*

What Jane knew about her father should have taught her those lessons, anyway. He had used her mother and abandoned them both. What little he'd left her when he died couldn't begin to make up for the pain he had caused.

Surely all men weren't like that, Jane had argued, but how would one know?

One can't, had been Grams's answer.

Jane busied herself transferring food into pie plates and bowls she wouldn't miss before Mrs. Tallon had a chance to return them. She tried to convince herself that her relationship with Adam was still business, the same as her relationship with George or the guests in the boardinghouse.

He was just one of the first men she had dealt with who was close to her age. Her responsibilities kept her from socializing much except with boarders, who tended to be older. That was the root of the attraction.

And why shouldn't she have a friend her own age? She was not quite twenty-two and couldn't remember ever having a friend. That was all Adam was. He had, after all, the beautiful Doreena. His interest in Plain Jane was probably because of their ages as well.

Or more likely because of his stomach.

At any rate, it was pleasant to have a friend, Jane decided, tackling the rest of the dishes once she had started a small pot of coffee. And she was safe from Adam because of Doreena.

Adam couldn't explain why he wished Jane had stayed. The boy and his mother were both cooperative and calm. He didn't need or even want her help.

He tried to put her out of his mind as he set the boy's leg and gave them instructions. "Don't put any weight on that leg," he finished. "I'll come out to take a look at it tomorrow. Let me know immediately if there are any problems."

"Thanks, Dr. Hart," Mrs. Tallon said. "I'll talk to the mister about how to pay you and get it taken care of as soon as possible."

"Can we go see Aunt Jane now?" Billy asked.

"How am I supposed to get you in there?" his mother responded. "I'll see if she can send a cookie home with us."

Suddenly the excuse to be in Jane's kitchen again was more than Adam could resist. "I'll carry him in, Mrs. Tallon. You can get the door."

"I always come see Aunt Jane when we're in town," Billy explained. "She likes little boys."

"I think you like her, too," Adam said, carefully supporting the injured leg as he lifted the boy into his arms.

"I shouldn't do it since I hardly know her," the boy's mother confided, "but sometimes I let Billy play at Miss Sparks's house while I do my shopping. She doesn't seem to mind and Billy's much happier that way."

Adam was a little curious as to what the ever-efficient-and-tidy Miss Sparks thought of having a little boy underfoot. He guessed she let Mrs. Tallon take advantage of her, the same way everyone at the funeral dinner had.

But then, she was the one who'd offered cookies.

Adam carried Billy into the kitchen, spotless now and smelling of fresh coffee. Jane had already positioned a chair with a pillow on it to support the broken leg. When Billy was comfortably seated, Adam stepped back to watch Jane. She gave the boy a hug then knelt down on the floor. "That's one fancy leg you've got now," she said. "Dr. Hart went to a lot of work to keep you from climbing trees."

"That's not why," the boy said.

Jane smiled at the child as she rose to her feet.

She served coffee to the adults and milk to Billy, and set a plate of oatmeal cookies on the table.

Jane was comfortable with the farm woman and talked easily about weather and crops. She was obviously a special friend to Billy. Adam watched her wink at the boy and slip him another cookie after his mother had said he'd had enough.

"The leg set all right, didn't it?" Jane asked him as Mrs. Tallon prepared to leave.

"It'll be fine. I just want to keep an eye on it for the next few days to be sure the splint keeps it immobile and there are no other complications."

"She can't keep bringing him into town," Jane said, wrapping some cookies in a napkin and tucking them into one of the boxes that sat by the door.

"I'll ride out to the farm," Adam said. He wondered what was bothering her. Mrs. Tallon had said they hardly knew each other. Was she worried about the boy or did she know something about the farm that he didn't? Her comment about pigs came back to him.

But her mind was on a different track. "He could stay here," she said.

Chapter Four

"Can I, Ma? Please," Billy begged.

Adam was sure his face showed his surprise. It would make it easier for him to check on the boy, of course, but Jane had just lost her grandmother. She hadn't yet caught up on the sleep she had lost during the woman's illness. A lively little boy frustrated by a broken leg would not make her life easier. He held his breath and waited to see what Mrs. Tallon would say.

"No," the mother said finally. "Your father will want to talk to you."

A new problem occurred to Adam. "No spankings until the leg is healed," he said.

Mrs. Tallon laughed. "You don't need to worry about that. But he'll likely be doing extra chores once he's healed."

Adam carried Billy back to the wagon, and Jane and Mrs. Tallon followed with the boxes of food.

After saying their goodbyes, Adam and Jane stood side by side and watched the wagon pull away.

"It was nice of you to offer to keep Billy," Adam said.

Jane gave him a sad smile. "It would have kept my mind off things," she said.

"You need to get some rest."

She shook her head. "I need to start dinner. I need to keep busy."

Adam watched her walk back to the boarding-house. Once she was inside, he returned to his own little house. He slumped into a chair and stared at his closed front door.

This house was way too quiet. He needed other voices and activity around him. He wished he were sitting in Jane's front parlor. Even if no one else was there with him, he would be able to hear the other boarders if they walked across their rooms. He would *know* that he wasn't alone.

He needed to convince Doreena to join him. He had already sent one brief letter describing his welcome to Clyde. He hadn't mentioned her refusal to come or his disappointment. He had been afraid he would say something he later regretted.

How could she think he would decide not to stay? Hadn't she listened to him at all? He could understand if she said she didn't want to leave her family and live in a comparatively primitive little community. But that wasn't what she'd said. She had said she was sure *he* would go back.

It didn't seem right that she should make him choose between the life he wanted and the woman he loved. He would get pen and ink and tell her so.

He was halfway to his feet before it occurred to him that that was precisely what he was asking her to do: choose between the life she knew and her love for him.

He slumped back into the chair. The difference, of course, was that he was the man. Tradition held that a woman left everything behind and started a new life with her husband. Doreena, however, would be leaving behind considerably more than most women. And getting far less.

Besides, he wasn't her husband yet. She could still refuse. It came down to the same question. Was he willing to give up his dream of practicing medicine on the frontier in order to be with Doreena?

With a sigh, he rose and moved to the desk. She had given him a year. Perhaps he could change her mind.

It took him most of the afternoon to write the letter, in part because he carefully chose each word, but also because of the interruptions. Two separate farm families stopped to meet him. They were in town anyway, they pointed out. Neither needed medical attention, but were merely checking him out, deciding, he supposed, if it would be worth calling on him if the need arose. He hoped he made a favorable impression. The fact that one of the farmers called him son did not seem like a good sign.

Finally the letter was written. He tapped the pen against his chin as he reread it. He had told about Billy Tallon, pointing out that without his help the boy might have been crippled for life. He had mentioned the Cartland sisters, brushing very lightly over their flirting. He hoped he had depicted them as amusing neighbors.

He had skillfully written of the old woman dying of pneumonia and of taking his meals at the boardinghouse next door without ever actually mentioning Jane. Now he wondered why. He hadn't been afraid Doreena would be jealous. He simply hadn't been sure how to describe her.

Thinking of his neighbor, he was considering arriving early for dinner when he had another knock at his door. "Come in," he called as he turned the letter over and placed the cleaned pen on top.

He stood as Rose Finley, the woman who had introduced herself at the funeral dinner, stepped across his threshold. She moved aside to admit a woman Adam guessed was just shy of twenty.

"This is my daughter Rosalie," Mrs. Finley said, smiling proudly as the girl curtsied. "This, my dear, is Dr. Adam Hart."

"Pleased to meet you," Rosalie said, with a tilt of her head that reminded him instantly of Nedra Cartland.

"She's been feeling poorly lately," Mama Finley continued. "I'll just wait here while you examine her in private." She plopped down in a chair and folded her arms, looking rather pleased.

Adam hesitated a moment before directing the young woman into the adjoining room. He closed the door behind them and leaned against it for a moment.

Rosalie stood in the center of the room, making a slow turn as she studied her surroundings. "I'd feel more comfortable if the shades were drawn," she said.

Adam opened his mouth to protest, but she had already stepped to the window that overlooked the street and was stretching to reach the shade pull. He quickly found a match and lit the lamp.

"Miss Finley—"

"You can call me Rosalie," she said, tossing a smile over her shoulder as she went for the other window shade.

"Rosalie," Adam began, becoming conscious of just how tightly the girl's dress fit when she stretched up on tiptoe.

"Yes?" She turned around and eyed him innocently.

Adam would have bet money there was nothing wrong with this woman except an overeager mother. Still...

"Have a seat," he said, indicating a stool that would bring her nearly eye-to-eye with him. "What seems to be the problem?"

"It's my throat," she said. "It's been sore lately."

Adam brought the lamp forward, positioned it on the table and turned up the wick. "Let's have a look."

She opened her mouth, and Adam turned her head until he got a good view of a very healthy throat.

"Your hands are warm," she said as he drew away.

"Thanks," he said, pretending not to notice the way she leaned toward him. "Have your eyes been watering? Do you have a runny nose?"

The pert little nose in question wrinkled distastefully. "No."

"Have you been coughing up any blood or phlegm?"

She shook her head, shuddering. "Don't you want to listen to my chest?"

Before Adam could catch her hands, she had loosened three buttons on her bodice. "That won't be necessary," he said.

"But you can do it, anyway," she said, leaning toward him again.

Adam was torn between the danger of continuing to hold her hands and the danger of letting them loose. Before he had made up his mind, she whispered, "Do you want to kiss me, Dr. Hart?"

Adam looked down into her eyes, barely six inches from his. "Not if you have a sore throat," he said softly.

He watched her as she considered her predicament. He expected her to admit that she had been lying, but perhaps she realized that she would then be admitting to throwing herself at him as well. After a moment she leaned away and lowered her eyes. He let her hands slip out of his grasp.

"My advice, Miss Finley," he said softly, "is to, ah, stop working so hard. Let things take their natural course."

"But Mama says—"

"I can imagine what Mama says," he said, moving away from her. "Don't let her push you into anything."

"Yes, sir," she muttered, gazing down at her lap.

Adam couldn't suppress a smile. "I think you'll be fine."

"Yes, sir." She slipped off the stool, still not looking at him.

"One more thing, Rosalie." She glanced up. "Button your dress."

Two bright spots of color appeared in her cheeks. She hastily refastened the buttons as she moved toward the door. Adam reached out and opened it for her. He followed her into the front room.

Mrs. Finley came to her feet and eyed her daughter expectantly.

"I think she'll be fine, Mrs. Finley," Adam said in his most professional voice. "Just go a little easy on her for a while."

Mrs. Finley looked from him to her daughter and back.

"That'll be a dollar, Mrs. Finley."

The woman opened her purse and carefully counted out the coins. With a last quizzical look at Adam, she herded her daughter out the door.

Adam turned back to the examining room and put out the lamp. He opened the shades and stood for a moment looking at the boardinghouse next door. Why should it seem particularly inviting now? The Cartland sisters weren't any more subtle than Rosalie.

Jane, however, was another matter. He could use a dose of her frankness after this afternoon. He grabbed his coat, tacked the oft-used note on his front door and was climbing her steps in a matter of minutes.

Jane gazed at the zinnias in the center of the table as her boarders and guests ate. When she had arranged the bouquet she'd thought she should take a few back to Grams. It was an odd feeling to realize that for just a moment she had forgotten she was dead. But maybe in a sense Grams was still with her, would always be with her.

Adam's words had eased some of her guilt over her grandmother's death, leaving her glad that the pain was over. Her sorrow now was for the loss of her closest friend and confidante. If Naomi said something outrageous to get Mr. Bickford's attention, with whom would she laugh with about it later?

At that moment, Adam chuckled over something that George had said. She hadn't been paying attention. When Tim Martin was there the conversation was always a little livelier, creating a diversion from her own thoughts. Tonight she had let herself drift away.

She turned her attention to the man beside her. He flashed her his boyish grin and whispered, "Welcome back."

"Sorry," she murmured. "My mind was elsewhere."

He nodded in understanding.

The Cartlands and George were arguing the relative merits of horseback versus buggies, and no one noticed the brief exchange. "What did I miss?" she asked.

"I asked about renting a buggy to get out to the Tallon farm tomorrow. It appears I may have to learn to ride horseback."

Jane smiled. "I've heard Mrs. Tallon talk about a creek that can make it impossible for her to get into town. Or to make it home if she gets caught in a rainstorm."

Adam nodded. "Mrs. Tallon made it in today, so I'm sure a buggy could make it out tomorrow. But that won't always be true."

Jane tried to look serious. "You need to learn to

ride, anyway, if you're going to live in the West. You'll be a cowboy before you know it.''

"I'll need to round up all those pigs I plan to raise.''

"Pigs?'' Naomi and Nedra spoke almost simultaneously.

"It's just a joke," Adam said, making an effort to hide his grin. Jane chewed her lip to keep from laughing outright.

"Well, I would hope so," Naomi said. "Pigs!''

While Naomi was adjusting to the notion that anyone would make a joke about pigs, Nedra seemed to have already forgotten it. "I'm not sure a gentleman should expect to learn to ride in one lesson," she said, shifting her worried gaze from Adam to George and back.

"To tell you the truth, I'm not sure, either," Adam said, still grinning. When Nedra's expression turned to alarm, he added, "I'll ask Mr. Knapp to loan me the oldest, laziest horse he's got. Besides, if I break anything, I can fix it. I'm a doctor.''

Nedra eyed him dubiously. "One would think that a doctor wouldn't take these things so lightly.''

"I'm sorry.'' He made another effort to be serious. "I'll be careful, really.''

His eyes were fairly dancing with excitement, Jane noted. "What time tomorrow are you planning on mounting your first horse?'' she asked.

"What time?'' He had turned his attention back

to his dinner, but paused with his fork halfway to his mouth.

Jane nodded. "I thought we should all turn out to watch the show—I mean, show our support."

Adam laughed along with George. The Cartlands seemed to have missed the joke. Jane wondered if Mr. Bickford was even listening.

Adam laid his fork back on his plate. "I may keep that information to myself. For modesty's sake, of course."

"But here's your chance to meet the whole town, Doc," George said. "They'll all turn out to watch a tenderfoot fall off a horse."

Adam laughed and the Cartlands scowled. Evidently deciding there had been enough merriment, Naomi and Nedra forced the conversation to other topics. Bickford excused himself, reminding Jane of the shirt with the missing button he had left for her in the parlor. The sisters followed him out of the room. George stood and, after assuring Adam that he would make the arrangements with Knapp's livery, left as well.

Adam had stood when the ladies did, but resumed his seat once they were gone. Jane wasn't sure if she should begin to clear the table as a hint that dinner was over or stay right where she was. She decided on the latter.

"You're excited about riding, aren't you?"

He nodded as a grin took over his face. "I've read

about cowboys and bandits since I was a kid. I may have to buy a pair of boots."

"And a pair of six-guns?"

"I don't think I'll go that far."

Jane watched him for a moment, marveling at how nice it felt to be near him. "What was your childhood like?" she asked abruptly.

"It was all right. What about you?"

Jane shrugged, not wanting to talk about herself. "It was all right, too, I guess. No horses or puppies, though."

"Me, either," he said. "But that's not as important as the future. And my future holds at least one ride on a horse."

"More than that if you don't break your neck."

"Right," he said. "And I haven't given up on that puppy yet, either."

"Or the pigs?"

He laughed. "I had a real paying customer today."

"Real money?"

"Real money. Rose Finley brought Rosalie by."

"Rosalie? Nothing serious, I hope?"

He shook his head. "Let's get the table cleared."

Jane stood as he did. "You don't need to help." Even as she said it, she was hoping he would stay. The kitchen seemed so empty with Grams gone. Fortunately, he shrugged off her token objection.

"Seriously," she began, as they each carried a

stack of dishes toward the kitchen, "when *are* you going to take your first riding lesson?"

"Seriously?" Adam sat his stack of plates on the kitchen table before he answered. "I don't think I'm going to tell you."

It felt so good to laugh. "I promise not to tell."

He seemed to think it over. She knew she needed to get started on the dishes. There was food to put away. There was also a companion in her kitchen and she watched him instead.

"I was considering an hour before dawn."

"No witnesses?"

"Right."

He returned to the dining room for more dishes, and Jane followed after him, laughing.

At the table he spun around to face her. "So. How good a horsewoman are you?"

"Me? I've never ridden."

"Never?"

"I grew up in the city. Besides, there was no money." Surprisingly, she didn't feel defensive as she said it.

"And no place to go," he added, nodding. "Same for me. But you've been out here awhile."

"Only four years. And it's still true. No money, and now no time."

"Ah," he said, flashing her a grin. "But now you have someplace to go."

She couldn't help smiling at his knowing nod. "Me? Where do I have to go?"

"To Billy Tallon's house. You can help me check his leg."

He turned to the table and began stacking dirty dishes, as if the matter were settled.

"Adam." Jane moved to the other side of the table, hoping her face didn't reveal how pleased she was that he wanted her along. "I don't know anything about broken legs."

"You can help me find the farm."

In a minute, nearly everything on the table was either in his stack or hers. Still they stood across from each other. Jane pretended to be interested in the table linen. "I've never been there, either."

"Come anyway." The plea in his voice brought her head up. "If I fall and break my neck, you can go for help."

She decided he was teasing. She lifted her stack of plates and silver and headed for the kitchen. "I can't go before dawn. I have breakfast to fix."

He fell in behind her. "After breakfast, then. I'll help you clean up."

She set her stack down and turned to the water she had left warming on the stove. What would it be like to ride across the prairie? With Adam? Not a good idea, she decided. Before she could frame another excuse, he spoke again.

"I promise to have you back in time to fix the evening meal."

She shouldn't have turned to look at him. She might have been able to laugh off the invitation. She might have been able to mention the cleaning that needed to be done. She might have even been able to convince herself she didn't want to go if she hadn't seen his face and realized he wasn't teasing.

"You need to get out of this house once in a while," he said softly. "You need to get some fresh air."

He was standing close to her, watching her with those caring blue eyes. She was keenly aware of her attraction to him, a pull that made her want to move closer, to touch him. The feeling was so sharp it was almost painful.

She spun away, finding the soap and shaving tiny flakes of it into the water, hoping he hadn't noticed her confusion. She hadn't yet found her voice when he added, "Doctor's orders."

She could hear the humor in his voice and wanted to sigh with relief. As long as they kept it light, she would be all right. It was when he turned serious that she was in danger.

Her grandmother's lessons came back to her. *Never let them know your weaknesses.* Somehow, arguing that she couldn't go seemed like an admission of fear, a fear that had nothing to do with horses and everything to do with her feelings for him.

"All right," she said, turning to give him a smile she hoped didn't appear forced. "Since it's the doctor's orders."

The grin she got in return was almost enough to make her relax. But not quite. As they washed and dried the dishes, she was careful that their fingers never touched. She leaned away rather than let their shoulders brush when he reached for a platter she had just washed. She made sure that she gave his gentle blue eyes no more than a quick glance.

When the kitchen and dining room were clean, Jane saw Adam to the door, then entered her bedroom. The big room was across from the parlor, with the door tucked under the stairs. She and her grandmother had shared it when they first arrived, leaving the upstairs free for paying guests. When Grams's illness had forced her into bed most of the day, Jane had cleaned out the storage room off the kitchen so she would be nearby. Finally, the poor woman had become too weak to move back and forth, and Jane had spent her nights in a chair at her grandmother's side.

It seemed odd to sleep alone in this room where she and Grams had shared so many conversations. She sat down on the bed and tried to imagine her grandmother beside her. "I would sure like to talk to you, Grams," she whispered.

But what would she say if Grams were here? "I felt a strong attraction to a man today. I felt it clear down to my toes. Yes, I know men will take advantage if they can. But I don't think he knows what I felt. I think I hid it from him."

Jane rose to get ready for bed. Here she was, imagining herself lying to her grandmother. Of course he had been aware of the attraction. Why else would he have talked so much about the beautiful Doreena if not to remind Jane of whom he had waiting? He didn't return her feelings, and he wanted her to know it. *She* wasn't beautiful. *She* wasn't rich. He wasn't in love with *her*.

She gazed at her image in her dresser mirror, wishing for soft blond curls and a tiny turned-up nose. "I was happier thinking he might take advantage," she muttered.

Adam couldn't keep his mind on the book he was reading. He kept thinking back on his conversation with Jane. Why had he talked so much about Doreena? The letter he had spent all afternoon writing had seemed like a reasonable excuse to have her on his mind, but it wasn't the truth. He had talked about Doreena in an effort to *keep* her on his mind.

For several minutes, when Jane was close to him, smelling of soap and fresh air and cinnamon from the apple pie she had baked, her cheeks flushed from their teasing, her dark eyes bright with laughter, he had forgotten about Doreena entirely. He had felt so guilty when he realized it that he had talked about her to make amends.

Only now he felt guilty for Jane's sake. It had probably sounded as if he were throwing his rich girlfriend in her face. Jane deserved better than that.

It occurred to him that if Doreena had come with him, he wouldn't have forgotten about her. Of course, if she had come with him, he wouldn't be taking his meals at the boardinghouse, let alone staying to help the hostess clean up. His relationship with Jane was going to change once Doreena joined him. While what Jane and he shared was nothing more than friendship, it wasn't going to look like that to Doreena.

Chapter Five

Adam sipped his coffee slowly, waiting for the others to leave the table. George and Bickford both gave him questioning looks as they left. But at least they left. The Cartland sisters seemed intent on staying as long as he did.

"Enjoy your coffee," Jane said. "If you don't mind, I'll start clearing the table."

Adam didn't miss the furtive glance she sent in his direction. She wasn't any more eager for the Cartlands to know their plans than he was. Last night they had joked about not wanting anyone to witness their first time on a horse. But the truth was Adam thought of his first horseback ride as a grand adventure, and he wanted Jane and not the Cartlands to share it with him. Since Jane had never ridden, either, it would be an adventure for her, too. He had a feeling that adventures were rare in her life.

"We could show you around town this morning,"

Naomi offered as Jane took a stack of dishes into the kitchen.

"Maybe later," Adam said, coming to his feet. "But right now I think I'll help Jane with the dishes."

"I'm sure that isn't necessary—I mean..." Nedra sputtered to a stop.

"Jane always—we don't—" Naomi closed her mouth and turned to her sister.

"There are plenty of towels," Adam said, "if you'd care to join us."

"What we mean," Nedra said, "is we'd be glad to help, but we really need to be picking out the fabric for the dress shop. I'm sure you and Jane understand."

"Yes, that's right. We need to be placing that order soon."

Both women were headed for the stairs before Jane returned for more dishes.

"Where did the Cartlands go?"

"Off to order fabric for their dress shop." Adam joined Jane in the task of stacking dishes.

"Ah," she whispered. "The phantom dress shop."

"Phantom? That sounds intriguing."

"They've been here a year and have yet to so much as arrange for a location for this shop. I think they're the ones shopping."

"For husbands," Adam said, remembering the

conversation he had overheard his first night in town.

"Can I let you in on a secret?"

"By all means," he said, following her into the kitchen.

"I think you're their first choice."

Adam had figured that out, too. "Not Bickford?" he asked, feigning surprise.

"I think the loser gets Bickford."

"I think whoever marries Bickford is going to feel that way."

It was fun listening to Jane laugh. Hers was a soft gentle laugh, as if she were trying not to be heard.

"Poor Mr. Bickford," she said.

"Poor Mrs. Bickford."

Jane shot him a grin over her shoulder. "You're taking the Cartlands' side?"

"Well, think about it. They came out west to find husbands. There were a lot of claims made a few years back that pretty women would find husbands in a matter of days. Think how they must feel after a year here."

"Discouraged, I expect. Until you moved in next door."

He could tell she was holding back a giggle. He uttered an exaggerated groan as he left with a stack of clean dishes for the dining room cupboard. He returned as quickly as he could.

She didn't turn to look at him when he came

through the door. "My bets are on Naomi," she said.

He groaned again. "Naomi of the orange hair."

"You should write Doreena to come rescue you."

She said it in the same joking tone, but it was like a splash of cold water to Adam. Doreena. Once again she had been the farthest thing from his mind.

They finished the dishes quickly. Adam tried not to let his sudden change in mood show. He should thank Jane for reminding him that he wasn't free. His conversation with her had slipped dangerously close to flirting. Which wasn't like him at all. Growing up in a house full of boys, he had always been a little shy around girls. Why did Jane make him feel so comfortable?

Or perhaps not so comfortable. Part of what he was feeling was sexual attraction, or at least awareness. And that he could blame on Doreena's absence. Jane was right; he should write Doreena to come rescue him, but not from the Cartland sisters.

Adam walked with Jane to the livery stable at the far end of Washington Street. He was more than a little self-conscious, after his earlier realization. He carried his medical bag between them as an excuse not to offer her his arm, though he felt derelict in not doing so. He didn't want anyone getting the wrong idea if they saw the two of them together. He didn't want to cause her any embarrassment.

Jane, however, didn't seem to expect anything from him. She walked beside him, commenting occasionally on this business or that as they passed. He told himself they were friends. They were neighbors. Jane was close to the patient he was going to see. He had no reason to feel guilty.

He told himself he was glad he didn't make her uncomfortable. He was glad she didn't feel the same attraction he had felt. His feelings were not injured by her ability to think of him as nothing more than a friend. That was what he wanted. That was the way it had to be.

By the time they got to the large wooden building at the end of the street, Adam was feeling inexplicably depressed. His mood brightened instantly at the sight of a saddled horse tied to the fence beside the barn.

Knapp met them at the door and introduced Adam to Molly, the saddled horse. Jane bartered away two places at her table for dinner, and Knapp left to saddle a horse for her. "I hope mine's smaller," Jane whispered to Adam.

Adam smiled down at her as he stroked the horse's nose. "I think they can tell if you're afraid of them."

"And will take pity on me, I hope."

"Come on," Adam coaxed. "She doesn't bite."

"You don't know that for sure," Jane said, but she inched her hand forward and stroked the silky cheek.

"Don't look now," she whispered, "but we're drawing a crowd."

Adam looked up the street and saw about a dozen men walking purposefully in their direction. As they gathered in the street he could hear a little of their conversation.

"Which horse you reckon Knapp picked?"

"That's old Molly. Where's the fun in that?"

"Miss Sparks is with him, boys. Hi there, Miss Sparks."

She answered and waved.

"Move back," someone shouted. "We don't want to spook the horses." The small crowd took a collective step backward.

"You be careful now, Miss Sparks."

Adam leaned toward Jane and whispered, "Now you know the real reason I invited you along."

Jane bit her lip to keep from laughing. It was an odd little habit he had noticed before. He tried to block it and the crowd out of his mind and concentrate on getting to know Molly.

A moment later Knapp walked out of the barn leading another horse. This one was spotted and every bit as tall as Molly. "So much for my wish for a short little horse," Jane said, and turned away.

While the horse had gotten only muttered reactions from the crowd, Jane's advance toward it caused an uproar.

"Damn it, Knapp."

"You gotta let Miss Sparks ride Molly."

"You ain't puttin' the lady on the General."

The General. Well, this was what he had been

expecting all along. Jane hadn't moved very far toward the new horse and Adam had only to reach out to catch her arm. "I think Molly's for you," he whispered.

"Do you think there's something wrong with the other one?" Jane asked. "You should take Molly, and I'll stay here."

"No, I think this is something I've got to go through sooner or later. You wait right here."

"Adam." This time she caught his arm. "Be careful."

He flashed her his biggest grin. "I wanted adventure."

Most of the crowd raised their voices in approval when Adam approached Knapp and the General. He could hear George Pinter's voice above the others. "Knapp, I told you no tricks."

"Ain't a trick," Knapp said mildly. "I ain't got that big a stable."

"What about Robin?"

"Feelin' poorly."

Knapp seemed just evasive enough for Adam to seriously doubt his honesty. However, he had a feeling that what was to come was a test of his acceptability. His riding skill wasn't in question as much as his ability to be thrown without making a fuss.

Still, the notion of actually staying on the horse, however unreasonable, had taken hold, and he was eager to throw his leg over the saddle and see what the General would do.

The General seemed placid enough as Adam stepped up to his left side. Attempting to mount from the wrong side was a common mistake of the tenderfoot, or so his reading had informed him. He was thinking how invaluable all those dime novels were as he shoved his foot into the stirrup. As his weight shifted from solid ground to the unstable support of the saddle, it occurred to him just how chock-full of misinformation those books might be.

Little-used muscles protested, but he pulled himself upward and settled into the saddle. He got his right toe in the other stirrup and started to relax.

Which was, of course, what the General was waiting for. Earth, sky, buildings and the cheering crowd blurred together in a dizzying blend. Adam's posterior was inches above the saddle and slammed back against it in a completely unpredictable rhythm. All he could do was hold on with his hands and his knees. Even his toes tried to curl around the stirrups.

As suddenly as it had begun, it ended. The General came to a standstill, shook his head, ruffled his mane and shifted his weight lazily from one side to the other.

The crowd, which had grown since it was last clearly visible, was cheering, but Adam barely noticed. Jane was staring at him, wide-eyed and pale. He reined the General around, and at the slightest nudge from his heels, the horse walked sedately toward her.

"Are you ready to go?" Adam asked softly.

She opened her mouth and closed it again.

Knapp walked up beside Adam and gave his leg a slap. "Nice work, boy," he said. "You just sit tight. I'll help the little lady aboard."

"Molly isn't going to do the same thing, is she?" Adam asked.

Knapp shook his head as he began shortening the stirrups for Jane.

George joined them as the rest of the crowd gradually dispersed. "I said no tricks, Knapp."

Knapp shrugged. "Couldn't resist once the folks gathered."

"He could have been hurt."

"Simmer down, George," Knapp said, casting Adam a grin over his shoulder. "Your boy made a fine showin'. The General'll behave himself the rest of the day."

"I think we'll get along fine." Adam directed his words to George, but he intended to reassure Jane as well. "Could you hand my bag up to me?"

George found the medical bag where Adam had left it beside the fence, and brought it to him while Knapp helped Jane into the saddle. With the bag slung on the saddle horn, Adam turned the General into the street and waited for Jane to join him. They waved at George and Knapp, then walked their horses across the bridge over Elk Creek.

"Do you know the way?" Jane asked, her voice a little shaky.

"George gave me directions. It shouldn't be hard to find." Adam was dying for her to say something about his brief rodeo ride. He was actually quite pleased with himself, especially considering the outcome.

Jane was quiet.

The horses plodded down the road at a steady, though rather slow, pace. Adam would have liked to try a faster gait, but didn't want to push his luck. Or Jane's.

"Having fun?" he asked after a few minutes.

"Actually, no."

"You're not scared, are you?" He moved ahead so he could turn and study her face. He was aware of just how pretty she was now that she had caught up on her sleep. In spite of her expression, he couldn't help but smile.

"Dismayed is more like it," she said, glaring at him.

"You don't have to worry. Molly isn't going to try to throw you."

"It's not that," she said, her big brown eyes softening. "I keep thinking of what might have happened."

He couldn't stop the smile. "You're still worried about me?"

"Don't look so pleased." There was a little of her old sass back in her voice. "How did you manage to stay on, anyway?"

"Seriously?" He waited for her nod. "If I could

have thought of a safe way to get off, I would have.'' He was very pleased to hear her laugh.

Jane was thoroughly enjoying the ride when they pulled up at the Tallon farm. Billy was sitting in a chair under a tree, his splinted leg resting on a pillowed sawhorse. Jane wanted to fling herself off the horse and run to greet the little boy, but her legs didn't want to cooperate.

Adam swung down, quite gracefully for a first-timer, she thought, and came to her rescue. She had to let him drag her out of the saddle, and then she had to lean on him because her legs wouldn't hold her. ''I guess I'm not cut out for this,'' she said.

''Give yourself a minute,'' he answered.

She felt his breath stir her hair. He was way too close and it did strange things to her nerves and muscles. She drew herself away even though she was half-afraid she'd fall flat on her face when she slipped free of his arms. She forced herself forward on trembling legs and made it to Billy's side. There she had the perfect excuse to crumble to the ground.

Adam, of course, was right behind her. He had turned the horses over to one of Billy's older brothers and greeted Mrs. Tallon on his way to the tree.

''Whatcha need that for?'' Billy asked, eyeing the medical bag.

''I don't need it, I hope,'' Adam said. ''What are you doing?'' He indicated the chunk of wood and pocketknife in Billy's hands. The boy's lap was covered with wood shavings.

"I'm learnin' myself how to whittle," Billy said.

Adam smiled. "Just don't cut yourself."

The boy groaned in disgust. "That's what Mama said."

Adam examined the boy's leg and asked him several questions. He seemed satisfied with the answers, and Jane and Billy beamed at each other.

Mrs. Tallon brought them glasses of cold water from the well, and in a few minutes it was time to ride back to town. Adam offered Jane a hand to help her rise. There was no polite way to refuse it. He kept one hand gently on her back as he walked her to the horses. It was such a casual gesture Jane wondered if he was even aware of it. She certainly was.

She tried her best to swing into the saddle without Adam's help, not as a show of independence, but to limit his very disturbing touch. She shouldn't have this reaction to him. Everything she was feeling was wrong. She had told herself this before. She'd thought she had settled it. Obviously, she hadn't.

Adam led the General a few feet away before he mounted. Jane was sure it was to put her at a safe distance in case the horse repeated his earlier performance. Jane held her breath, but the General stood quietly while Adam mounted, then obediently followed his commands.

"Maybe he's only cranky first thing in the morning,'' Adam said softly as they rode away from the farm.

''Maybe you let him know who's boss,'' Jane suggested.

Adam appeared to think it over. ''That's not why,'' he said, in a perfect imitation of Billy.

That night at supper Adam was the center of conversation, or more accurately, his ride was. Mr. Knapp brought it up first, with George providing additional details. The Cartland sisters were quite free with their admiration and scolded Knapp severely for putting their nice Dr. Hart in danger.

Adam seemed to be at once amused and embarrassed. Jane was glad her own first ride was nearly forgotten.

She was passing around bowls of bread pudding when George pulled out his pocket watch. ''I almost forgot. I got a letter today from the Children's Aid Society of New York City. I intend to pay some calls tonight, round up a placing board.''

''What,'' wondered Nedra, ''is the Children's Aid Society?''

''It's an organization that finds homes for orphans from the streets of New York,'' George said.

Naomi wrinkled her large nose. ''That would not be an easy task, if you ask me.''

Nedra nodded at her sister. ''Can you imagine?''

It was clear to Jane that they were imagining dirty little urchins, and not with any compassion, either.

Her interest was so centered on watching the women exchange grimaces she was surprised to hear Adam speak up.

"Orphans, you said? They're sending city orphans out here?" His attention was turned to George, giving Jane a chance to study him. He had more than a passing interest in the subject. In fact, he seemed excited by the prospect of orphan children arriving in Clyde.

"Orphans and half orphans. Some are immigrants," George added. "I'm to form a placing board to round up prospective families. They like to have the children placed with farm families, mostly. They believe farm life and labor is conducive to healthy minds and bodies. 'Course, nobody at the Children's Aid Society ever worked on a farm."

Adam's eyes lost some of their enthusiasm. "So they become indentured servants."

George pursed his lips. "Not in theory, anyway. Families are expected to treat the orphans as their own, and farmers work their own kids. They have to. It's just that farmers are more likely to think another pair of hands is worth the extra mouth to feed, while the businessmen in town don't usually need more unskilled labor."

Adam raised an eyebrow. "What about adopting the children out of love?"

George grinned. "I think we need you on the placing board. You can be in charge of finding loving families."

Adam didn't seem at all taken aback by the suggestion. In fact, he seemed eager to begin. "I don't know many of the families here yet," he said, but it was more to himself than to George.

"You can get to know them fast this way."

Adam smiled, evidently happy to have his only objection answered so quickly. "Of course I'd be happy to help."

"That's one down already. The orphans will come into town by train with their sponsors and be introduced at the Methodist Church, where the families can pick out a child."

Jane remembered the few times she had ridden on a train and the bone weariness that followed. "Surely they won't go immediately to the church," she interjected. "They'd be welcome here for refreshments before the presentation."

George nodded. "That's kind of you, Jane. We'll plan on it. Adam, you want to come with me while I try to round up the rest of the board?"

"Sure," he said, rising as George did. "Terrific dinner as always, Jane."

She smiled in thanks at the compliment and watched the men walk out together, already discussing whom to call on first.

The Knapps left next and the boarders shortly after. Jane remained at the table for a few minutes, telling herself she wasn't disappointed. She was happy Adam would be helping to find homes for the orphans. She was happy he and George were becoming good friends. She certainly didn't need any help with the dishes.

She gathered a stack of plates and went to the kitchen, conscious of every clatter of china, every clink of the silverware. Her own footsteps seemed to echo though the rooms as she made trip after trip between the kitchen and the dining room.

How many times had she done this task alone, trying to be as quiet as possible so as not to disturb Grams, listening all the while for any sound from the tiny bedroom? The silence in that room was almost palpable.

This, she told herself, was the reason she had wanted Adam to stay. He filled her kitchen with talk and laughter. He kept her from thinking about her loss.

Maybe he had done her a favor tonight. She needed to think about her grandmother. Oddly, Jane had accepted Grams's death but not her absence. With her gone, the burden of running the boarding-house fell entirely to Jane. This she could accept; the last few months she had done all the work herself. But she had relied on Grams when it came to any decisions. Now she had to make those by herself, also.

Her first decision, she thought as she slid a stack of plates into the soapy water, would be what to do with the little room off the kitchen. She hadn't set foot in it since they had wrapped Grams in a blanket and carried her away.

She swallowed a lump in her throat. Grams would want her to move on. Jane could convert the room for storage, but she didn't have that much to store, and the kitchen was well appointed with cupboards.

She considered moving into the room herself, leaving her own room available to let. That would mean a little more money, and she needed every penny. The trip to Kansas City had used up all their savings. Making the payments on the house wasn't going to be easy.

It made perfect sense, she decided as she scrubbed a platter clean. It also gave her something definite to do to improve her situation. The fact that there was already a vacant room upstairs kept her from feeling as optimistic as she might have otherwise.

And trading two meals for the rent of a horse hadn't been a wise business decision. Of course, she could hope that Mrs. Knapp had enjoyed the evening away from her own kitchen enough to talk her husband into doing it again, this time for the usual fee.

Even if they never returned, Jane had a hard time regretting her excursion with Adam. It had been exciting and exhilarating. He took such pleasure in little things it was impossible not to enjoy them herself. In fact, she loved watching his face as he talked to the others around the table. She loved teasing him the way she teased the little boys that came to her back door to beg for cookies.

There was something special about the young

doctor, something that pulled her toward him, that made her want him to be with her every moment.

Her hands stilled on the plate she was drying. She was dangerously close to falling into the trap her grandmother had described so many times. Always before Jane had thought her mother was foolish to have fallen for her father's sweet words. Foolish, as Grams had said, for trusting another with her whole life.

Suddenly Jane understood her mother and was terrified.

Adam lit a lamp and started another letter to Doreena. He had mailed a letter that morning and counted the days until he could expect to receive one in return. Tonight he had so much more to tell her.

He wrote about the horse the livery had provided, hoping it sounded humorous. It was always a little difficult to guess what Doreena would find funny. He wrote about the orphan train, and the part he would play in placing the children. As he wrote, he found himself emphasizing the importance of the board to the community and minimizing the orphans themselves.

He wanted to tell her how he felt when he thought about those little children abandoned by parents, whether by choice or by death. How it felt to yearn for someone, anyone to care about you, to say you were worth the food it took to keep you alive.

Somehow, he couldn't imagine Doreena understanding. She had been loved and pampered since
the day she was born. She put great store in family
lineage, in ancestors that had arrived before the Rev-
olution.

The thought that Jane would understand came to
his mind. Jane had been orphaned, too, sometime
along the way, or she wouldn't have been so close
to her grandmother. Jane wouldn't be embarrassed
by his desire to help these children find new parents.

He shook off the disloyal thoughts. Doreena was
the one he should be sharing this with. He wasn't
giving her enough credit. She was an affectionate,
loving girl. She would understand how hard it was
to live without the very things that she found important.

Of course she would.

He took up the pen, glared at his hand until it quit
trembling, and put his feelings down on paper for
Doreena to read. If he thought of Jane now and then,
as if it were she who listened, that was simply because he valued her friendship.

Chapter Six

Immediately after the breakfast dishes were done, Jane started on the little room. She tore the bedding from the bed and put it all to soak in tubs of soapy water. She wasn't going to think about how distant Adam had been at breakfast. She wasn't concerned that he had work to attend to and couldn't stay to help with the dishes.

She carried two chairs to her backyard and slung the narrow mattress over them to air in the sun. She hadn't ever liked the thought of one of her dinner guests staying to help. Grams would never have allowed it. Grams would have had a thing or two to say about their friendship, besides.

Jane's main weakness right now was loneliness. Had Adam become aware of it? Perhaps not or he might have stayed this morning to help with dishes and talk.

Which brought her back to the question that had plagued her all through the meal. Why was he so distant? What had happened between the ride to the Tallon farm and breakfast this morning to change everything?

She stomped back into the house and into the little room. She flung open the windows and began gathering up the few personal items that had made their way in from the big bedroom at one time or another. She shouldn't be worried that she had said something wrong. She shouldn't be concerned that her realization of the night before might have caused *her* to treat him differently, and *his* behavior had merely been a reaction to it.

She *should* be glad that things had stopped before...

Before what? Before he took advantage of her? This was where Grams's warnings were hard to associate with Adam. Jane couldn't quite picture Adam seducing her and disappearing. He lived next door.

And there was Doreena. Yet Jane realized that Doreena was protection only if Adam had a conscience, which Grams said men didn't, except sometimes when it came to business.

It had all made so much more sense before she actually fell in love.

When that thought surfaced Jane almost dropped the armload of pictures and books she had gathered. She couldn't be in love. Could she?

If she was, it explained why she wasn't thinking straight, and it meant she couldn't trust her judgment. What she needed to do, she decided as she hurried through the house toward the big bedroom, was put some distance between herself and Adam. This morning had been a good start.

She dumped her burden on the bed and sat down beside it. She also needed to keep her mind occupied. And she knew just the task. She had done very little spring housecleaning because of her grandmother's illness, and had neglected the house almost entirely during the past month. She would start with the vacant room upstairs, then the parlor, dining room and kitchen. This room could be made ready to rent once the upstairs room was occupied.

First, her grandmother's things needed to be moved into the attic. Surely there was an empty trunk up there. Jane lit a lamp, went upstairs and then took the steeper, narrow steps into the attic. She hadn't been up here in this part of the house in a long time.

A few pieces of discarded furniture cluttered the room, decorated with a fine layer of dust and spiderwebs. Three trunks lined one wall, the trunks she and Grams had brought with them, filled with all they had owned.

She moved a wobbly chair aside and opened the first trunk. She had expected to find it empty, but a faintly familiar dress lay only inches below the top of the trunk. She pulled out the dress and held it up to the lamplight. It was a silver blue, and seeing its color clearly triggered her memory. It was her mother's dress.

Now she remembered watching her grandmother

pack away her mother's things, telling her that when she grew up, she might want to wear her mother's dresses. The dresses had come west with them, then had been forgotten.

She would check the other trunks—at least one ought to be empty—but first she wanted to see more of her mother's possessions.

Her mother had led such a short sad life, and Jane had hardly known her. She didn't know what she hoped to learn, but she pulled the dresses out one by one and tried to remember her mother wearing them. None of them seemed like anything she would want to wear herself.

Beneath the dresses were a few personal items— a hand mirror; a pair of shoes, the leather stiff and cracked; a Bible in similar condition; a set of blocks that had been her own. Jane smiled as she lifted one of the brightly painted pieces. They had been made from scrap lumber by one of the frequent boarders at Grams's. Each side was part of a picture, making six different puzzles to be solved with the nine blocks.

There was also a small wooden jewelry box with a string tied around it. She lifted it out of the trunk and realized the string wasn't holding it closed, but rather held a little note. She slipped the note out from under the string and recognized her grand-mother's handwriting.

"Hanna's jewelry box. Key lost. Nothing of value inside."

Nothing of value to anyone except the daughter

who was missing both women so much. Maybe there was a cheap broach or ring that she could treasure because it had been her mother's. She carried it to the lamp and examined the tiny padlock and clasp. It shouldn't take much to pry it loose.

When the dresses were repacked carefully in the trunk, she carried the jewelry box down to her kitchen. She was right; it took a simple butter knife to pry loose the tiny tacks that held the clasp to the wood.

Inside she found a packet of letters, tied with a faded satin ribbon. The top one was addressed to Mrs. William Sparks, her mother.

Jane left the packet in the box and closed the lid. Sometime soon she would read the letters. Sometime when her emotions weren't quite so raw.

A young boy came to get Adam shortly after breakfast. The mother of the house was ill. She had been feeling poorly for some time and was intending to get into town to see him. That morning she had had barely enough strength to drag herself out of bed and had sent one of her boys to town.

Adam made note of the six solemn faces in the outer room before he slipped behind a curtain to see his patient. When he reached a diagnosis, he broke the news to her as gently as he could. He left her crying into her pillow and reported to the family. Only the youngest, a girl of about six, was happy to hear there was another child on the way.

Adam returned home to find Rose Finley waiting for him. "This is Rosetta," the woman said.

"Another sore throat?" Adam asked.

Rosetta shook her head.

Adam directed her toward the examining room and, while she preceded him inside, he took a last look at the mother watching proudly from her seat across the room.

Adam closed the door and turned his attention to Rosetta. "You're younger than Rosalie, aren't you?"

"Only eleven months," she said. "I'm taller, though."

"I see. What seems to be the problem?"

The girl gave him what was probably supposed to be a sultry gaze. "I don't know what's wrong, Doctor," she said. "That's why I'm here to see you."

"All right," Adam said, not moving an inch farther into the room. "Describe your symptoms."

"Well, let's see." She began strolling around, running a delicate finger over this and that. "I feel...lethargic sometimes and nothing can hold my interest. Other times I feel filled with nervous energy." She brought her hands together at her breast. "It's simply impossible to sit still and do my stitching or to concentrate on a book. Do you know what I mean?"

"Have you tried acting?"

"What?"

"Never mind. Is there more?"

She took a deep breath. "Well…I lose my temper at my sisters, which I never used to do."

Sisters, plural? Oh, wonderful.

"Really, I'm a very even-tempered girl, but lately their childish arguments and their silly games just irritate me. Mother says I'm not myself. Do you think I'm ill?"

"No, I think you're young."

She gave him a perturbed scowl.

"I mean, everything you've described is normal for a girl your age."

She took a couple of predatory steps toward him, and he leaned against the door. "You mean a girl who is becoming a woman?"

"Uh, Miss Finley…"

"Can we talk more about that? My becoming a woman, I mean."

"I don't think so. Your father's the one you should talk to." Adam had the door open before she could protest. He assured the mother that the daughter was fine, but charged her a dollar anyway, hoping to discourage her from throwing any more daughters at him.

He saw the ladies to the door and stepped out onto his porch to watch them stroll down the street, their heads together in whispered conversation. He turned to look toward the boardinghouse before he went back inside.

He felt guilty about not staying to help this morning. He had been able to convince himself that there was nothing inappropriate about his feelings for Jane until he had written to Doreena last night. Then it had occurred to him that his feelings for Doreena seemed to be changing, and his relationship with Jane was probably to blame.

If he hadn't spent so much time with Jane, he wouldn't be thinking that Doreena's conversation always centered on herself, that her laugh was not quite natural and that she was always aware of someone watching her, and acted accordingly.

He loved Doreena. He had told her so. She was the most beautiful woman he had ever seen. She had agreed to marry him in spite of her parents' misgivings. He had no intentions of betraying her.

And wasn't comparing her to Jane a form of betrayal? It had to stop. In last night's letter he had asked Doreena to join him—begged her, actually, as Jane had suggested. What he should do, he decided, was picture Doreena at his side every moment he was with Jane.

With that new theory to test, he walked to the boardinghouse and up the steps. It would be easier to picture Doreena here than in his own house, anyway.

Yes, Doreena would like this house, he thought as he came through the front door. She would like the long open stairway. He could imagine her making a graceful descent as guests waited in the parlor below.

At that moment Jane, her arms wrapped around a huge bundle of bedding, started down the stairs. She was peering around her burden when she saw him and jumped. Afraid she was about to lose her balance, Adam dashed up the steps to catch her. With an arm around her waist he helped her to the bottom.

"Thanks." She sounded slightly breathless. She had taken more of a scare than he'd realized.

"You ought to throw the bedding over the railing instead of trying to carry it down the stairs."

"I know," she said, walking toward the kitchen. "I forgot to move the hall table, though, and I was afraid of knocking over the vase."

Adam followed her, noting the delicate vase of violets as he went by. Would Doreena have thought of the vase? He had trouble picturing her carrying bedding at all. Which wasn't fair. Doreena wasn't going to be running a boardinghouse, he reminded himself.

"Did I see Rose and Rosetta leave your house a moment ago?" Jane asked over her shoulder.

"That's right," he said, following her through her kitchen and into the backyard. Jane dropped the bedding on the ground and separated a sheet, which she shoved into a huge tub of soapy water. More snow-white sheets snapped in the breeze behind her.

"Did Rosetta catch something from Rosalie?"

"Not exactly." He tried to imagine Doreena standing beside him watching Jane do her laundry. It wasn't easy.

"Not exactly?" Jane straightened and started the sheet through a ringer attached to the tub.

He stepped forward to turn the crank. He couldn't stand by and watch her do it all herself. "Watch your fingers. No, actually, neither girl has anything catching. Just a mother a little overanxious to see them married.''

When Jane looked up, she was chewing on her lip.

''Go ahead and laugh. I would, too, if they didn't scare me so much.'' Once he heard her laugh he couldn't stop his own. ''How many more are there, anyway?''

''Just one. She might be able to give Nedra and Naomi some serious competition.''

''Very funny.''

She dropped the sheet into a tub of clear water. ''I thought so,'' she said. ''Her name's Rosemary and I guarantee you'll like her.''

Adam groaned. This was a conversation he was supposed to imagine Doreena listening to? Jane continued to wash sheets and pillowcases and he continued to help where he could, becoming more and more conscious that this was not what he should be doing.

It wasn't the laundry that bothered him. He'd rather be helping with someone else's work than doing nothing. What he shouldn't be doing was enjoying Jane's company. He needed to put Doreena firmly between them and keep her there.

''Doreena will really love your house,'' he said, looking up at the high windows and steep roof. Even from the backyard it was pretty.

''Thanks,'' she said. ''Grams fell in love with it the first time she saw it.''

"Not you?"

Jane shook her head. "I wanted to go home."

"Home was better than this?"

She laughed. "No. Home was a falling-down shack in the worst part of town. We took in boarders there, too, to make ends meet. But home was familiar."

"Well, Doreena will be jealous," he said, coming back to his point. "She's used to better than the little house I'm renting."

Jane fished a sheet out of the rinse water and sent it through the ringer again. "She won't care about the house," she said, smiling at him as she caught the wet sheet in the basket.

Adam followed her to the clothesline and helped her spread the sheet over it. The wire sagged from the weight, making it possible for him to see Jane over it. "What makes you think she won't care about the house?"

"She won't if she loves you."

Her eyes had locked with his, and he was struck by how pretty she was, with her big brown eyes so warm, her lips parted in a gentle smile. Gradually her eyes widened and the smile faded. He was touched by how vulnerable she looked in the instant before she turned away.

At that same instant he wanted to swear. Doreena wasn't between them as firmly as he had hoped, even when they were talking about her. But the sheet was. It flipped up and slapped at him, making him back away. He watched Jane from a distance for a moment, feeling a need to apologize but unsure for what.

"I ought to get back," he said, finally. "I forgot to put the note on the door."

She turned and smiled. "See you at dinner, then."

After the easy dismissal, he walked across her yard and his and entered through his back door. For some odd reason he couldn't imagine Doreena following him.

Jane watched Adam leave and let the forced smile fade. If she believed her grandmother, which she thought she did, she should be warning Doreena away, not feeling jealous. More evidence that she wasn't thinking clearly.

But how could she when he looked at her the way he had? And what had he read in her face? Her weakness wasn't her loneliness. Her weakness was Adam Hart. And it was possible that he knew it.

Over the next several days, Jane threw herself into her housecleaning. Adam sat next to her at meals twice a day but he never stayed to help. She made sure of that. When he offered, she told him she had some other task she needed to do before she started the dishes. Eventually, he quit offering.

After a few cold days that changed the leaves to gold and brown, the weather turned warm again, making it possible for Jane to continue airing out curtains and bedding.

Adam was seeing more patients now, she noticed.

Not that she was watching his house. He lived right next door. She couldn't help but notice.

He stopped by nearly every day with questions about one family or another, sometimes because they were patients, but usually because they had asked to be considered as homes for the orphans. Jane was always busy with the cleaning, and he always pitched in for a few minutes.

Since the school term wouldn't start until November, Jane still had an occasional small visitor. Suzy Gibbons skipped in during one of Adam's visits. Jane was on a ladder removing the parlor curtains, and Adam was trying to convince her to let him take her place.

"Whatcha doin', Aunt Jane?" queried the youngster.

"Aunt Jane is trying to break her neck," Adam answered.

"Why you wanna break your neck?"

"Adam," Jane scolded, forgetting for a moment that she should speak to him no more than necessary, "don't lie to little girls."

She tried to ignore Adam's laugh as she released the rod from its bracket and let the curtains fall to the floor. "I need to clean the curtains," she said as she backed down the ladder.

"Did you get jelly on 'em?"

There was Adam's laugh again. "No, they're just dusty," she answered, trying to ignore him completely.

Suzy scowled at the curtains, then shrugged off

the dust as unimportant. "I came to see if you had any cookies. Mama didn't make any 'cause I was bad, so I'm running away."

Jane responded as casually as she could, "This is the third time, isn't it?"

Suzy pinched her eyes closed and scratched the end of her tiny nose. She raised the fingers of her other hand to keep count. "There was the jelly on the curtains, the torn dress, the broken egg…and this time." She opened her eyes to look at her fingers. "Four."

Jane tried to keep her voice stern. "And this time was…?"

Suzy's brow furrowed. "This time was nothin'!"

"Suzy?"

Suzy stomped one little leather-clad foot. "Do you got any cookies or not?"

"Not until you tell me."

She seemed to think it over for a minute. "Mama says I sassed but I was just sayin' what's what."

Adam came forward and knelt down at Suzy's level. "What does your mama do when you break the rules?"

Jane wanted to push him aside and tell him to let her handle Suzy. How was she supposed to fall out of love with him when he displayed so much concern for a little girl?

However, his charm seemed to be lost on Suzy. She scowled at him. "Who are you?"

"I'm Dr. Hart. I'm a friend of Aunt Jane's." He tossed a questioning look over his shoulder, but Jane only gazed at him. She knew what he was getting at. She didn't think there was anything wrong at the Gibbons's house, but Adam might get different answers than she had.

Suzy pointed at Adam. "If you're her friend, *you* ask her for cookies."

"I think I can talk her into cookies," Adam said. "But I want to know what your mama does."

"Grown-ups always want *somethin'*," the little girl grumbled. "She sends me to my room and forgets I'm there."

"How long does she keep you in your room?"

Suzy's eyes got big. "For weeks!"

"Suzy," Jane said in a warning tone.

"Well, sometimes clear 'til supper."

"And that's all she does?"

Suzy leaned toward him, her cheeks turning pink. "She plays with the dumb ol' baby. She makes the baby laugh while *I'm* stuck in my room. They're *glad* I'm gone."

Suzy's lower lip trembled. She brushed past Adam and ran into Jane's arms. Jane gathered her up and let the little girl bury her face in her neck. "I know it's hard to be a big sister."

Suzy mumbled something that was too muffled to understand.

"She started running away when her sister was born," Jane explained to Adam as she carried the little girl toward the kitchen. "I give her a cookie and send her home."

"This time I'm not going back!"

Jane set Suzy on a kitchen chair. "I can't make you, I guess," she said as she got the tin of cookies. "But that seems kind of mean."

"They're the ones who's mean."

"Maybe," Jane said. "But remember your first day of school? If it hadn't been for Mandy next door, you couldn't have done it. Who's Becky going to go with her first day? Mandy will be done."

"I don't care." Suzy reached for the tin, but Jane hadn't opened it yet, and Suzy had never been able to make the lid cooperate with her little fingers.

"And who's going to teach Becky how to climb a tree? Your mother?"

Suzy actually laughed. "She can't climb a tree."

"Becky'll have to find some boy to teach her."

Suzy made a face. "Yuck!"

"What's wrong with boys?" Adam asked.

Jane bit her lip. "So, are you going back?"

Suzy let out a long, low groan. "I guess so. But I still think she's stupid."

Jane popped the lid off the tin and held it out for Suzy to choose a cookie. "She'll get smarter. Just give her some time."

Suzy grabbed a cookie and slid off the chair. She left a little trail of crumbs all the way to the back door.

"Doesn't giving her cookies encourage her to run away?" Adam asked once the little girl was gone.

"I don't know," Jane said. "As long as she comes to me when she runs away, her mother knows where to find her."

Adam sat in the chair Suzy had vacated and reached for the tin. "So you've talked to her mother?"

Jane turned to start some coffee. "She told me Suzy started throwing tantrums when her sister was born. Any little scolding can set her off. The baby, of course, is never in trouble for anything."

"I was afraid she was being punished for what sounded to me like accidents."

Jane sat down across the table from him. She shouldn't be doing this. She had work to do. But she was so tired a cup of coffee might help her get through the rest of the day. "The jelly was spread on the curtain with a knife. The egg was broken against the wall, and the dress she tore was her sister's.

"But I wondered, too, the first time. She was a little vague on what she had actually done and what her mother's reaction had been. There wasn't a mark on her, though, except a scrape on her shoulder from going through the window."

"I guess I'm starting to imagine things, after interviewing families for the orphans. I just don't like to think of any child being mistreated."

Jane got up to gather the cups for the coffee. "There's only so much we can do, Adam. We can't interfere with the parents."

"What are you saying?"

Jane couldn't turn to look at him. She watched the pot instead. "Not all children are treated well by their parents. I let the ones who aren't come for cookies, too, or stay the night while their parents cool off. That's all I can do.''

"Tell me who they are." He rose and moved to stand beside her. She could feel his warmth, smell his clean masculine scent.

Jane shook her head. "If they ask for an orphan, I'll tell you. But otherwise, the children wouldn't want you to know."

He was quiet—thoughtful, she supposed—while she waited for the coffee to brew. She was torn between wishing he'd return to the table and wanting to lean against him.

His fingers skimmed the side of her face, tucking a stray lock of hair behind her ear. "I think you're overdoing this housecleaning project."

She reached a shaking hand up to her tingling cheek. "How can a house be too clean?" Her voice held the slightest quiver.

"What difference does it make how clean the house is if you work yourself to death?"

She grabbed up the coffeepot and brushed past him to the table. *Don't turn your concern on me. I'm not prepared to handle it.* She forced a laugh. "That's a little dramatic, don't you think?"

"You look more exhausted every day. Having curtains with no dust isn't worth that."

Jane took a sip of coffee, trying to decide how much to tell him. "I have to work hard all day in order to sleep at night," she said finally.

"You're still grieving for your grandmother."

"Yes." That was part of it, of course, but financial worries were a larger part. And dreams about Adam himself. But she couldn't tell him that.

"I could give you something to help you sleep," he offered.

"No," she said. "I think this is something I need to work out myself."

She took a sip of coffee and changed the subject. "I have another boarder. A young man named Ferris Wood looking for business opportunities. You'll meet him at dinner."

"I suppose I should let you get back to work," Adam said.

Jane passed him the tin of cookies and said with a smile, "Don't scatter crumbs like Suzy did."

Chapter Seven

Adam had taken to walking to the post office every day. So much time had passed without a word from Doreena that he was surprised when a letter was actually waiting. He hurried home to read it, feeling an odd sort of dread as well as anticipation. After he had gone through it twice, he tossed it on his desk and paced across the room.

It was the kind of letter he had expected her to write when he first arrived. It was filled with descriptions of all the functions she had attended, all the friends she had seen here or there. Somehow, after the dozen letters he had sent her, he had expected a little more.

He had thought she would say something about coming west, even if it was a refusal. He had thought she would at least comment on his practice or something that he had written to her.

Maybe she hadn't gotten his letters. He hurried back to the desk and skimmed the letter again. No, there it was. "I've received your many letters and find them a comfort, as I miss you very much."

Well, at least she missed him.

Moments before, Adam had been hoping there would be no interruptions. Now he found himself relieved when the door opened, at least until he turned and saw Rose Finley enter with her third daughter.

"Good morning, Mrs. Finley," he said, trying to sound cheerful. "This must be Rosemary."

"Why, yes." Mrs. Finley was evidently pleased he had been asking about her family. "Rosemary." She gave her daughter a shove. "Meet Dr. Hart."

"How ya doin', Doc." Her mother cleared her throat, and Rosemary tried a mock curtsy.

Adam couldn't resist a smile. Jane was right. He liked her already. "What seems to be the problem?"

"You know, I think I feel just fine, now. Sorry to bother you, Doc." She turned to leave, but her mother effectively blocked the way.

"Now, we wouldn't want your condition to go untreated, Rosemary, in case it's serious."

Rosemary hung her head and turned back around. "Which way?" she asked.

Adam pointed toward the examination room. Once she was out of her mother's sight, Rosemary perked up. "Isn't Mama something?" she asked as soon as the door was closed.

"There's nothing wrong with you, is there?"

Rosemary shrugged. "I'm supposed to show you

the scrape on my knee if I can't think of anything better. You want to see it?''

"Might as well.''

Rosemary hopped up on the stool and flipped up her dress without displaying the least bit of bashfulness. "I've been puttin' Mama off for weeks, then this happened, and I couldn't do it anymore. It's a honey, though." She rolled down her stocking and unwound a white bandage. "I got it getting Riley's ball off the roof. That's my brother. He was scared to try to climb the trellis. I wouldn't have gotten hurt if I'd been wearing pants. Try to explain *that* to Mama.''

Rosemary had taken most of the skin off the lower part of her knee. Adam knelt on the floor to get a better look. It seemed to be healing nicely. "Did you treat it with anything?''

Rosemary bent forward and poked at the edges. "I put honey on it. Mama wanted to wash it with vinegar, but I lied and said I already had.''

Adam rose to get some ointment that might be a little more effective than honey or vinegar. "You lie to your mother at lot, do you?''

"Oh yes! We all do. It's the only way to live with her. You should hear what my sisters told her happened in here.''

Adam winced. "I think I can live without that.''

Rosemary shrugged. "I know what really happened 'cause they told each other. We never lie to each other.''

He returned to the girl with the jar in hand. "I'm more curious what your mother told you."

Rosemary laughed. "Mama wants you for a son-in-law. You should be flattered. She's letting you have your pick of the litter."

Adam spread the salve gently on the wound. "So, what are you going to tell her?"

"First I'm going to tell her that you're awfully old."

Adam looked up to see her smiling down at him. "You don't know how nice it is to hear that."

She laughed. "You should tell her this is terribly infected, and it'll cost a lot to take care of it. In fact, I should stay with Aunt Jane 'til it heals or you'll have to cut off my leg."

"Just what Aunt Jane needs," he muttered. He got a clean bandage and rewrapped the knee.

"At least tell her you put twenty dollars' worth of stuff on it. And tell her," she continued as she rolled her stocking back into place, "that you think I'm dumb or ugly or something. Mouthy! She'll believe that."

Adam helped her off the stool. "I think you're the pick of the litter, but you're too young to leave your mama."

Rosemary scowled. "That's not going to help me for very long!"

Mrs. Finley seemed pleased to see him smiling when he escorted Rosemary back into the front room. She paid the dollar and nickel quite cheerfully, and promised she'd be seeing him again soon. Rosemary rolled her eyes at Adam before she followed her mother out the door.

Jane thought young Ferris was fitting in nicely. He had found employment at George's bank and seemed to be settling in as if he expected to stay awhile. With all four rooms upstairs filled, she needed to prepare to move out of the downstairs bedroom at a moment's notice. Tonight after supper she would move all the things in Grams's dresser into one of the trunks in the attic. Her own dresser could be quickly moved into the room off the kitchen when she got another boarder.

Jane was rushing around putting the final touches on dinner when Adam arrived. He didn't come to the kitchen to see if he could help like he used to. The last several days he had waited in the parlor with the rest until she called them for dinner.

Still, she knew the moment he arrived. Even before she heard his voice, she recognized his step. She had thought the distance she had forged between them would help keep her from thinking of him. It hadn't worked that way at all.

He even seemed to be cooperating with her plan. He spent less time with her, and when they were together the conversation rarely got personal. Not since he had told her she was working too hard.

Jane took a last inventory of the table, straightened her spine, put a smile on her face and went to call the guests. She stood in the hall for a moment admiring her parlor. The furniture gleamed with polish and the windows sparkled. Fresh cockscomb and strawflowers graced every tabletop. She was sure the curtains and the rug looked a shade brighter for having been thoroughly cleaned. Grams would have been proud of her.

And proud of her, too, for not letting anything come of her attraction to Adam. He was watching her, of course. He was the only one who noticed her presence.

"Dinner's ready, everyone," she said.

They trooped to the table and took their usual places. Even Mr. Bickford was on time. The conversation centered on the activities of the town and was intended mainly for their newest member. The Cartland sisters vied for Ferris's attention, much to the obvious relief of both Adam and Mr. Bickford.

Jane only half listened. She was already planning how to get Grams's things up to the attic. What chore could she tackle tomorrow? Mr. Bickford's room hadn't been cleaned yet; he spent a lot of time there writing and hadn't been receptive to the suggestion. Perhaps he would be willing to name a day when she could do a thorough cleaning. Once it and her bedroom were done the house would be as clean as she could make it.

The others were leaving the table when Adam said softly, "Let me stay and help you."

He hadn't asked for so long it startled her.

"That's not necessary," she said quickly. "I was going to sort through some of Grams's things before I start on the dishes."

Adam shook his head. "You can go through her things after the dishes are done. Or better yet, put it off until tomorrow. I want to talk to you."

As soon as the others had left the room, Jane gathered a stack of dishes. Out of the corner of her eye she watched Adam do the same. It felt a little like old times, except now she knew she was in love with him and understood just how foolish that was. Her only defense was to pretend that nothing was different from the first time he had stayed to help.

"What did you want to talk about?" she said as they walked to the kitchen.

"I think you're working too hard."

"You told me that before. Want to wash or dry?"

"Jane, I'm serious. You're too pale. You've lost weight. There are shadows under your eyes again."

There was no use denying any of it. "You sure know how to compliment a girl," she said, hoping her smile looked real.

"Are you getting any sleep at all?"

"Of course, I am." She turned away to gather more dishes. He trailed behind her.

"Look, maybe it's none of my business, but I thought we were friends."

"It's kind of you to worry," she said. "But I'm fine, really."

"No, you're not fine." He took the dishes from

her hands and put them back on the table. "This place is too much for you to handle alone."

A suggestion was one thing. Telling her what she couldn't do was another. Especially when he was the primary cause of her sleepless nights. "I'll have you know I've run this boardinghouse for years."

"With your grandmother's help. You're alone now. You need to consider doing something else."

"Like what?"

"I don't know. Sit down for a minute, Jane."

"I have work to do." She gathered up more dishes and headed for the kitchen.

He followed her, of course. "What I'm getting at is that if you do decide to give up the boarding-house, I'd like to buy it."

That stopped her dead in her tracks. "You want to buy my house?"

She let him ease her into the chair that stood just inside the kitchen and lift the stack of plates from her hands. "I'd have to arrange something with the bank, or maybe Doreena's parents."

He turned away from her to begin washing the dishes. He seemed to be talking to himself more than to her. Or perhaps it was the buzzing in her ears that produced that impression. He wanted to buy her house. For Doreena. Was there any truth in his declaration of concern?

"I just wanted you to know there are other options besides working yourself to death at the boardinghouse. I've seen you with children. You'd make a wonderful teacher.''

The logical part of Jane's brain told her teaching was a good idea, since she loved children and would never have any of her own. Another part of her brain had no interest in logic. Female teachers weren't allowed to marry. Was that why he'd suggested it? Pretty women found husbands in a matter of days, he had said. What did that make her? Such a poor catch she might as well give up? *He* didn't know she had vowed never to marry!

He continued to talk about the house and Doreena, citing what she had been used to. Jane gathered he had received his first letter from her and hadn't been encouraged by what she had said. Jane was in no mood to be sympathetic.

Yet part of her yearned to explain. While she couldn't tell him her foolish longings were keeping her awake, she was tempted to tell him about her financial difficulties. She couldn't sell him the house even if she wanted to because she didn't entirely own it. *That* was why she worked so hard. She needed to maintain her reputation for running the best boardinghouse in the area.

Grams's warnings kept her lips sealed. That would be telling him her weakness. Or her second greatest weakness. And what might he do with it if he truly wanted the house? One rumor of a less than healthful meal and her reputation could be ruined.

She would lose the house, and he could make his arrangements with the bank.

She told herself that Adam would never do such a thing. However, since she was blindly in love with him, she didn't trust her own judgment. She'd have to rely on Grams's advice.

"I can't sell the house, Adam," she said, rising and walking to the drawer that held the tea towels. She didn't dare look at him; her pain was sure to show in her eyes. "This is my *home.*" *Or almost.*

Whether he accepted that or not, Jane wasn't sure. At least he quit describing how much Doreena would like her house. It was a wonder, she decided, that he didn't suggest she stay on to cook and clean for Doreena. She realized she was drying a platter a little more forcefully than was necessary and tried to quit torturing herself with the prospect.

Half of the dishes were done before he spoke again. "Please consider slowing up a bit with the housecleaning."

"I just want everything done before the children come."

Adam turned to smile at her. "These children aren't going to notice."

"No," she admitted, "but their sponsors might." They were prospective customers, of course. But that wasn't all there was to it. While Adam interviewed families and judged whether they could take a child or not, she felt a strong desire for him to find her worthy, too.

* * *

Adam knew he had hurt Jane's feelings. He was truly worried about her. More than the symptoms of exhaustion that he had mentioned, there was a sadness about her that tore at his heart. But it was natural for her to miss her grandmother. The house must be full of reminders of happier days and terribly sad ones. He had thought she might welcome a chance to get away from it. He had hoped she might welcome a chance to do something less taxing as well.

Instead she thought he had insulted her. Questioned her abilities. Dismissed the importance of her home. He hadn't meant to do any of those. He had only meant to help her.

And himself. The house seemed like the only thing that might possibly tempt Doreena to join him. He described it in his next letter, stating that he was looking into the possibility of buying it. It wasn't exactly a lie, though there was no way he could persuade himself that it was entirely the truth.

All's fair in love, he thought as he took the letter to the post office. *Or better yet, desperate times call for desperate measures.*

A few patients, interviews with prospective families and meetings with the other members of the placing board kept him busy during the next several days. The day the orphans were scheduled to arrive, he received Doreena's response.

He found his hand shaking as he tore the end off the envelope. He skimmed the letter quickly, stared at the last line for several seconds, than started at the beginning again.

Since Doreena had no wish to live in the middle of nowhere and his letters indicated he had no intention of coming back home, she thought it was best that they break their engagement. He would thank her later, once he got over his broken heart.

She went on to say she had already informed her parents and they were taking it very well. Of course they were. They were probably delighted.

As soon as she had made the decision and, evidently, the announcement, she had thrown herself into social activities, hoping to ward off any talk of melancholia over the broken engagement. Everything was working out splendidly for her, as she was certain it soon would for him.

Doreena, it seemed, had been swept off her feet by someone "of her own class," as she put it.

Adam carefully refolded the letter and slid it back into the envelope. He should feel desolate. Doreena had not only broken their engagement but had already found someone else. He waited for the pain to come, for the shock to set in.

He took a deep breath and as he let it out realized all he felt was relief. The worry of how he could possibly make her happy was suddenly lifted from his shoulders.

His next thought was that he wanted to tell Jane, not only about the letter but his reaction to it as well. Jane, however, would be busy making final preparations for the orphans' arrival. She wouldn't welcome his intrusion.

She barely spoke to him anymore, anyway. She seemed to think he was out to steal her house, or some such nonsense. He found himself worrying about her more each day. He wished he knew what to do to help her.

The boardinghouse was sparkling when Jane welcomed the sponsors and their fourteen charges inside. The children ranged in age from a sweet-faced sixteen-year-old girl to a small boy of only two. The little one promptly wandered into the parlor, climbed up in a cushioned chair and fell asleep.

The other children lined up their little suitcases in the hall and placed their coats on top, then gathered around the table, where they ate sandwiches and carrots and drank milk. One small girl stayed very close to Mrs. Elder, one of the sponsors. At first Jane thought the girl was shy, but soon decided that the sponsor was keeping close watch on the girl. When one of the other children drew Mrs. Elder's attention, the little girl crept away. Jane watched her quietly slip behind the heavy drapes that hung on either side of the large window.

Mrs. Elder looked around for her charge. "Where did Peggy go now?" she asked the other children. The oldest girl pointed to the curtain.

"Little Miss Peggy," the sponsor said, hunkering

down in front of the curtain and drawing it aside to reveal the girl, "what are you doing back there?"

Peggy let herself be drawn away from the wall and back into the group. "Don't you want some more to eat?"

"Peggy's," said the little girl when Mrs. Elder offered her a sandwich. Peggy tried to shove it into the tiny pocket sewn on her apron.

"Peggy," Mrs. Elder said gently, "you have to eat it now."

Peggy, the sandwich clutched in both hands, sat down on the floor and scooted under the table. Jane could see her sitting cross-legged, placidly eating the sandwich.

Mrs. Elder sighed. "I wondered about the wisdom of bringing her. She has too many strange habits. Besides, she's probably close to four and doesn't talk except for saying her name. If anyone takes her, I expect they'll be asking us to come back and get her in a matter of days."

Jane bent for another look at the little girl. She seemed completely content, looking out through the forest of legs. One of the older boys leaned over to grin at her and received a smile in return.

After everyone had eaten, Mrs. Elder asked for a room for the six girls to change into their better dresses. The seven boys were left under the supervision of the other sponsor, Mr. Holt, and Jane led the way to her bedroom. While the girls changed, Jane went across the hall to check on the baby. He was curled up in a tight ball. Jane couldn't resist gathering the little one into her arms. He let out a soft sigh and settled into her shoulder.

To think of this precious little boy being orphaned or abandoned at such a tender age brought tears to her eyes. "Someone will want you," she whispered into a tiny ear. "Anyone would want you."

He stirred, stretched, then stared at her with bleary eyes.

"Are you hungry, sweetheart?" she asked.

He simply stared.

Afraid that he would become frightened when he realized a stranger was holding him, she carried him into the dining room. Mr. Holt was checking each boy, making sure their shirts were buttoned and tucked in and their hair was neat.

"Charlie's awake," one of the boys volunteered. Several of the boys greeted the baby, who turned away from Jane to stare at them.

Jane took a sandwich from the plate and placed it in the child's outstretched hands. She poured a fresh glass of milk and took one of the recently vacated chairs. With Charlie on her lap, she helped him take occasional sips of milk, and watched Mr. Holt coach the boys.

"Stand up straight. Look people in the eye. If you don't like the looks of a family that asks for you, say so. You're good boys. There are plenty of people who can use you. You try to pick someone who'll be good to you."

Seven boys nodded their heads.

"If you see someone watching you, someone who looks kind and happy, do like I told you. Go ask if they want to be your mother or father."

With a sigh, he ran an eye over each of the boys again. "You're next, Charlie."

Charlie turned at the sound of his name, but continued to eat. Holt put his hands on his hips and looked down at the boy. A smile slowly spread across his face. Charlie laughed and offered him a bite of the crumbling bread.

"We'll brush you off when you're done, and you'll be ready for the show. If we can keep you until we get to the church, that is." For Jane's benefit he explained, "We had two offers on the train."

"His hair's all over the place," a freckle-faced boy said.

Jane smoothed the downy hair, but it defied her efforts.

"His hair is hopeless," Holt said, smiling at the older boy.

Mrs. Elder and two of the girls joined them. "Did Peggy come in here?" Mrs. Elder asked.

Jane shook her head. "She may have gone into the parlor."

"Alex, go look," Holt directed.

"I didn't hear the front door open so she's sure to be in the house," Jane assured them.

"Try under the bed," one of the boys suggested.

"Oh, heavens," Mrs. Elder said, turning back up the hall. "She'll get herself all dirty."

Jane hid a smile in Charlie's soft hair. She wouldn't get dirty in this house—not right now, anyway. This, she would tell Adam, was the reason she had cleaned.

In a few minutes Mrs. Elder led the rest of the girls out of the bedroom. Peggy had evidently been retrieved from under the bed. Mrs. Elder, her hand firmly wrapped around the little girl's wrist, said, "I believe we'll go on over to the church. I'd like to have the children inside before people start arriving."

Jane handed Charlie to the oldest girl while the children filed out. Mr. Holt thanked her before he followed, urging a couple of dawdlers to a faster pace.

Jane sat for a moment, thinking about Peggy and Charlie. She had planned to attend the presentation and had prepared a cold supper that she was going to leave for the boarders. Now she wished she had made no such arrangements. Fixing the usual big meal would keep her mind off the little children.

She asked herself if it would be better to see the children leave with their new families or sit here and wonder about them. With a sigh, she stood to clean the table. She knew Adam had worked hard at selecting good families. Anyone asking for a child today without having already applied would have to be approved by the board. She didn't have to worry for these children.

The more she thought about it, the more she knew she wanted to be there. She quickly cleaned up after the children and laid out the buffet, carefully covering each dish with a cloth. She couldn't dismiss the urgency she felt even as she left the house and hurried around the other folks making their way to the old city hall, which now served as the Methodist Church. In the large meeting room, she took a seat near the front even though spectators not applying for children were urged to sit in the back. She needed to be as close to the children as possible.

Chapter Eight

George came out and quieted the audience. After introducing the members of the placing board, all of whom were seated to one side, he explained the procedure, then turned the program over to the sponsors. A row of chairs had been arranged in front of the altar, and, as Mr. Holt led them out, the children took their places. The oldest girl carried Charlie and settled him on her lap. Peggy, her hand in Mrs. Elder's, brought up the rear.

Mrs. Elder helped the little girl into her chair and stood behind it, her hands resting on the child's shoulders. To Jane, Peggy looked very uncomfortable. She squirmed in the seat and tried to get her shoulders out from under Mrs. Elder's control. Mrs. Elder bent and whispered to the girl, who cringed away.

Mr. Holt glanced at Peggy, but went on with the introductions. He called each child's name and, while he or she stood, gave a brief description of that child's background.

By the time it was Peggy's turn, she seemed on the verge of rebellion. Mrs. Elder stood her up and, kneeling beside her, tried to hold her in such a way that she faced the audience. Mr. Holt had no more than stated she was Peggy, last name unknown, when she wailed, clutched her stomach and bent forward so forcefully Mrs. Elder's best efforts weren't enough to keep her from falling to the floor.

Jane leaped to her feet. Adam, she realized, was already hurrying toward the child. Jane couldn't merely watch from a distance. She made her way forward as quickly as possible.

Holt, after a nod from Mrs. Elder, directed the other children back to their seats. "I'm sure it's nothing to worry about," he said. "Will the families who have picked out a child please come forward now?"

The noise faded into the background as Jane knelt beside little Peggy. "What's wrong with her?" she asked. Peggy was on her back now, tossing her head from side to side. Her lips moved as if she were whispering to someone. Her eyes were tightly closed.

Adam, kneeling on the other side of the girl, shook his head. He removed his suit coat and folded it for a pillow. Peggy tried to roll onto her stomach and hide her face in the coat. Adam gently rolled her back. She pulled the coat around her head instead.

"Peggy," Jane said gently, trying to coax her out from under the coat. "Tell us where it hurts, sweetheart."

The girl clutched the coat all the tighter.

Adam gently probed Peggy's stomach. With her face covered it was hard for Jane to gauge her reaction. She didn't cry out again, at least.

Still Jane was terrified for the little girl. She had seen enough death recently. This child had to be all right. "Adam?" she whispered.

Their eyes met. He looked as concerned as she felt. He shook his head. "I don't know. I don't think it's anything serious. Maybe it was something she ate."

"She ate at my house," Jane said, horrified at the prospect.

Adam actually grinned. "We can rule that out, then."

Jane smiled in gratitude. She had to avert her eyes before she gave herself away. She was too frightened to guard her emotions. "Come on, sweetheart," she coaxed again. "Come out and tell us what's wrong."

Peggy shook her head, coat, arms and all.

George and Mrs. Elder stepped up beside them. "Adam," George said, "nobody's asked for this little girl."

"We can hardly be surprised," Mrs. Elder said sadly. "She's such a strange little thing."

"Has she done this before?" Jane asked, hoping for reassurance that nothing was truly wrong.

"Not exactly this," Mrs. Elder said.

"What happens if no one wants her?" Adam asked.

"When children aren't chosen, we like to leave them in temporary homes until permanent ones are found. At least that's what we usually do. I don't see that there's much chance anyone will want this one, especially if she's sick. I suppose we'll take her back with us."

"If she is ill that may not be wise," Adam said.

"Let me have her," Jane said impulsively. She had always loved children. This could be her chance to have one as her own.

Mrs. Elder raised an eyebrow. "A single woman isn't exactly what the society is looking for, but if the local placing board agrees we have no objection."

"Can you leave her long enough to join us for the vote?" George asked Adam.

"I'll stay right here," Jane promised, "and call you if anything happens."

Adam nodded and came to his feet. In a moment only Mrs. Elder lingered nearby.

"Peggy," Jane cooed. "Everybody's going home. You can come out now."

A muffled buzz emanated from the wadded coat.

Jane leaned down to listen. "She's whispering," she told Mrs. Elder.

Mrs. Elder nodded. "I've never been able to understand her. I doubt if she's really saying anything at all."

"Peggy," Jane whispered loudly, leaning close to where the little arms held the coat closed. "Come out so I can hear you."

The placing board convened in the corner behind the pulpit. "Just so everyone knows," George began, "Jane Sparks has asked for the little girl, Peggy. We all know Jane, I think, so we can skip the discussion. Vote yes or no. We need a unanimous vote to let her take the child."

Adam was torn as he listened to the older man speak. No one could possibly love a child more than Jane. Only a blind man could miss the longing in her eyes when she looked at little Peggy.

Besides, he didn't like the idea of Peggy going back to the orphanage, especially if she was sick. And even if she wasn't, it would be hard to convince anyone who had seen her this evening to take her.

Still, Jane wasn't well, either. She was working herself into exhaustion. Adding a child, especially one that might need extra care, wasn't a good idea. And wasn't good for the child in the long run, either.

Because he had been standing a little to the side in order to make up his mind, it fell to him to cast the final vote. He hadn't even listened to the others, but assumed, since the voting continued, that they had all voted in favor. In good conscience, he could not. "No," he said.

The committee was quiet for several seconds. George looked stunned. "Well," he said finally. "That does it, then. Do you want to tell her?"

Adam hadn't thought that far ahead. The pain of that prospect must have shown on his face.

"I didn't think so." George's expression softened almost immediately. "I'm sure you have your reasons, son."

He gave Adam an understanding nod as he went by. It didn't help much. In the same way, knowing he was right didn't make him feel any less guilty. He followed the rest of the committee back toward Peggy and Jane. As much as he hated to witness Jane's disappointment, he needed to hear exactly what George told her.

He didn't tell her much. She looked up and read it in his face. "They won't let me take her, will they?" she asked.

George shook his head. "I'm sorry, Jane."

The placing board and the two sponsors stood in a rough circle around the girl. Jane remained on the floor. "So what happens to her?"

"I guess we send her back with the sponsors," George said.

Adam knew he had stayed in the background long enough. He took his former place on the floor with Jane, though he couldn't look her in the eye. "I don't think she should travel until we know for sure she's all right. Can either of you stay in town a couple days?'' he asked the sponsors.

They glanced at each other. ''I'm afraid we have appointments on our way back,'' Holt said. ''Do you think there's any chance you can find someone who'll take her?''

They had selected several more families than they needed, yet the extras had been willing to walk away with no child rather than ask for this little girl.

He was about to voice these thoughts when George answered, ''I say we give it a try. Agreed, boys? I further suggest that, since the girl may be sick, we send her home with Dr. Hart, on a temporary basis, of course, while we look for a permanent home.''

The sponsors seemed thrilled with this idea, giving Adam no chance to protest. He probably wouldn't have anyway, he decided. In a way it was what he deserved. ''Come on, honey,'' he said, lifting Peggy to a sitting position. Several hands reached out to help the girl up.

Peggy groaned and squeezed her eyes shut. This return of the earlier pain alarmed Adam. He caught her up in his arms and stood. She barely weighed anything. Maybe in her half-starved state she had eaten too much of Jane's good food.

The others moved off and let him carry the girl away. Jane hurried around him to open the door. She had his suit coat over one arm and Peggy's little suitcase and coat in hand. He would have been surprised if she hadn't come with him.

"Did you get any information out of her?" he asked as Jane tucked the little coat around the girl.

"Mrs. Elder says she doesn't talk, but I'm sure she was saying something," she answered as they hurried the two and a half blocks to his house.

"You couldn't understand her?"

"I couldn't hear her," Jane clarified. "She whispers. If it's really words, she's whispering very fast."

"I'm afraid she could have appendicitis," Adam warned her. "If she does, I'm going to need an assistant. Do you think you can do that for me?"

"I'll do my best, Adam, but I don't think that's it. She seemed to be getting better until the board came back."

They had reached the house, and Jane held the door. Adam carried Peggy directly to the examination room and laid her gently on the table. Jane wasn't two steps behind him.

If it was appendicitis, they might not have much time. Peggy held her fingers close to her face, twisting them together rapidly. Her lips were moving just as fast.

"Something's distressing her, but I can't tell if it's pain," Jane said.

"Watch her face. Tell me if she has any reaction." Very gently he began probing the child's abdomen.

"I don't think she likes it," Jane said. Her voice didn't hold the urgency he was feeling. He looked up to discover her leaning very close to a tiny ear.

She whispered something, and the girl went still. Her eyes darted around the room as if she were seeing it for the first time. In the silence that followed even Adam heard her whisper, "Gone?"

"All gone," Jane said softly. "Just Dr. Hart and Aunt Jane."

Peggy tried to push herself up to a sitting position. Jane gave her a hand. "All better?"

"If she isn't sick," Adam said, feeling both relieved and confused, "what was wrong?"

"Stage fright," Jane said, smoothing the little girl's dress. "What's this?" She fished into the apron pocket and withdrew a piece of carrot. She held it out to Peggy.

Peggy smiled and took it, poking it back into her pocket.

He remembered the cries and groans from the theater. "All this fuss for stage fright?"

Jane laughed. "It was quite a severe case, I admit, but that's all it was. I watched her when she first came on the stage. She wanted to turn away from everyone. When Mrs. Elder wouldn't let her, that's when she cried."

"And hid in my coat."

"She's been trying to hide since they got here," Jane said. "Behind the curtains. Under the table. Even under my bed."

Adam eyed the little girl, who now sat calmly on his examination table, looking around curiously. "The next few days ought to be interesting," he said.

"And all you wanted was a puppy," Jane teased.

Her smile didn't hide the hurt in her eyes. "I'm sorry, Jane," he said. He put his arms around her, intending only to comfort her, but found his lips skimming across her temple.

She stepped away from him. "I understand."

He doubted very much if she did. Before he could try to explain, she spoke again. "I laid out a buffet for the boarders before I left. Why don't I run over and fix us a tray? You and Peggy can get better acquainted."

As he watched her walk away, Adam felt a momentary panic. He wanted to shout at Jane to hurry back. He turned to Peggy and found her watching him curiously. "I'd know what to do with you if you were sick."

She blinked at him, and he smiled. "Here," he said, lifting her down from the table. "Go take a look around."

Jane was on her way out of her house with the tray when she turned back and gathered extra blankets from the linen closet. Adam would have to find some place for Peggy to sleep, and she wanted the girl to be comfortable.

She found Adam sitting in one of the chairs in his

front room, elbows on his knees and his chin in his hands. He was so deep in thought she wasn't sure he noticed her return. "Where's Peggy?" she asked.

He straightened and scowled up at her. "Under the desk. Any suggestions would be welcome."

He looked so perplexed she had to laugh. "Why don't we join her?"

"What?"

Jane crossed the room and set the tray on the desk. She peeked in at Peggy and whispered a loud, "Hi, sweetheart," as she pulled the chair out of the way. "Can Adam and I have a picnic down here?"

Peggy didn't respond, but she didn't look alarmed, either.

Adam helped Jane spread the blankets on the floor behind the desk. He seemed a little skeptical of the whole idea. "Didn't you like to crawl into small places when you were little?" she asked as she sat down.

Adam handed her the tray and joined her on the floor. "Not that I remember."

"A place like this," she said, indicating the little space Peggy occupied, "can be your own little house, or a cave or maybe a rabbit hole."

"I don't think she's playing," Adam said. "I think she's hiding."

"Then we'll hide with her. Look what I have." She uncovered the tray and held an apple wedge out to Peggy.

Peggy took the offering and shifted until she

found her pocket. Holding it open with one hand, she dropped the apple wedge inside.

"Don't put that in your pocket," Adam said, reaching in to tickle the little girl. "Put that on your skinny ribs."

Peggy giggled and batted his hand away.

"I think that means she's full. What about you?"

With the tray on the floor between them, they shared what was left of the buffet—bread and beef, corn relish and apples. They tried to talk to Peggy as they ate but got nothing more than smiles out of her.

Jane was aware of how close Adam sat, of every time his knee touched hers or his hand brushed against her arm as he reached for something on the tray. She didn't want to think about how tempting he was.

"Who do you think will take her?" Jane asked.

"I need to talk to you about that."

Jane shook her head. She didn't want to hear why the board felt a single woman was unsuitable. George had probably mentioned how precarious her finances were. Which meant Adam knew now, too—something she didn't even want to consider at the moment.

"Look," she said, drawing his attention to the little girl again. "I think we need to find a place for her to sleep."

Peggy was slouched in a corner, her chin rolling on her chest.

"I'll put her in my bed and sleep down here."

Jane scooted out of the way so Adam could reach Peggy. She used her hand to shield the child's head from the edge of the desk as Adam drew her out.

"The first thing you better do," Jane said, "is wake her up and take her to the outhouse."

The look on Adam's face told her this hadn't occurred to him at all. She chewed on her lip as she watched him. "Are you waiting for me to volunteer?"

"I was trying to decide if one knee or two was the more effective position for begging."

Jane laughed and took the sleepy child out of his arms.

"I'll be upstairs turning down the bed," he said.

"Cleaning the room is more like it," she teased. "I've had enough boarders to know how men keep house."

She hoped the joke hid what she was feeling. The disappointment at being rejected by the placing board was still a sharp pain, but it was easing somewhat. No one else had wanted Peggy. The sponsors hadn't taken her with them. There was still hope, however small, that she could convince the board members to reconsider their decision.

But while that thought stayed in the back of her mind, something else was beginning to overshadow it. She had just spent an hour or so in Adam's home. She was soon to enter his bedroom. While the little girl's presence kept everything proper, she couldn't help the thoughts that entered her head.

She scolded herself for her foolishness. She wasn't a child and this wasn't make believe. If she ever forgot herself and got too close, Adam had only to mention Doreena to remind her of her place. And, she vowed, if he didn't, she would.

Peggy wanted to be carried back to the house and immediately rested her head on Jane's shoulder. Jane carefully closed the back door behind them and started toward the stairs. She knew the house well, but she hadn't been inside since Adam had moved in. She was very much aware of the fact that she was heading for his bedroom.

Adam was waiting for them. "Let me carry her up the stairs," he said.

"She weighs next to nothing," Jane said, reluctantly letting Adam take the girl out of her arms.

"I know," he said, "but the stairs are steep."

Jane let him get a few steps ahead of her before she followed. She hadn't exactly been invited up, but she was determined to see the child settled comfortably for the night. Besides, she didn't want to go home just yet.

The entire floor was one room, with sloped walls and dormer windows. Adam had lit a lamp that filled the room with a soft, warm glow. His narrow bed was neatly made with a corner turned down. Books lined the lower part of nearly every wall. Jane saw several thin spines that were probably his Wild West novels. She found herself more curious about his books and possessions than she should have been.

She shifted her attention to Peggy. However, Peggy was with Adam, and Jane had been trying not to think about him. That was impossible, anyway, especially considering where they were.

Adam sat Peggy on the side of the bed and knelt to remove her shoes. She turned and looked at the pillow for a second, then crashed down onto it. Adam set the shoe aside and went after the other.

"I found a nightgown in her suitcase," he said softly. "Do you think it's worth the trouble?"

Jane stepped forward and brushed the child's fine hair away from her face. "No," she whispered. "But we better get the apron off her or that apple slice will attract a swarm of gnats by morning."

Adam placed the second little shoe beside the first. "I wouldn't worry about gnats," he said, resting one hand very casually on Jane's shoulder. "The spiders'll take care of them."

Jane looked at him sharply to find him smiling mischievously at her. "If you think I'm taking on your house next, you're mistaken."

"That hadn't crossed my mind."

Peggy had curled up on her side, her face turned toward them, and Jane was able to reach behind her and untie the apron. She slipped the ruffled bib over Peggy's head and gently pulled the rest out from under her.

"Want to try for the dress?" he asked.

"It's that or iron it in the morning."

"I know which I'd choose." He leaned over the bed and undid the buttons that ran all the way to the hem. "This shouldn't be too difficult." He slipped the sleeve off Peggy's right arm, then paused, considering the left arm, curled under the little girl's head.

Jane chewed her lip as she watched him. She was sure he was weighing the wrinkled dress against an unhappy child if he woke her. She couldn't leave him to his dilemma for long. She slid her hand under Peggy's head and raised it an inch off the pillow. Adam worked quickly to free the dress from the now accessible arm.

As soon as Jane laid Peggy's head back on the pillow, she sighed and rolled over. Adam sighed, too. Jane covered her mouth to stifle a laugh. "We better leave her alone before we wake her," she whispered.

Adam nodded. He pulled the covers up over the child. His fingers lingered a moment on a little pink cheek, then he drew Jane away from the bedside.

Jane's body reacted instantly at being so close to him. Instead of stepping away, as her mind suggested, she leaned closer, turning her face toward his. His lips were mere inches from hers. He didn't seem at all surprised to find himself in this position. In fact, he was bending closer!

Jane jumped away, nearly staggering. She shook out the little dress she still held and laid it over the back of the suitcase. After emptying the pocket, she laid the apron beside the dress. Her illogical mind was already wondering what would have happened if she had let him kiss her.

She forced herself to think of Peggy and, hoping her voice didn't betray her, asked, "Will she be all right up here alone?"

"She'll be fine," he assured her, "as soon as we quit fussing over her."

Though she was still reluctant to leave the little girl, she let him direct her to the stairs and preceded him down. She didn't want him to have to drag her away; she couldn't afford to let him touch her. Downstairs she added the apple slice and carrot to the other few scraps on the tray to be tossed to her chickens.

Adam stood very near her as he lit the lamp. She should step away. She should take her tray and go. She shouldn't be thinking of an excuse to stay. Was she hoping for a repeat of what had nearly happened upstairs?

The letter that lay on the desk beside the tray caught her eye as the light filled the room. She wanted to cry even as she reminded herself of her vow.

"You heard from Doreena," she said, hoping she sounded pleased.

"Yeah, I did." He definitely sounded pleased. Jane swallowed a lump in her throat as he brushed past her to gather up the blankets from behind his desk.

She might as well dig the knife in a little deeper. "Did she say when she's coming?"

He went around the desk and started spreading the blankets on the floor again. "Actually, she's not," he said.

Jane moved to help him with the blankets. An excuse, she knew, and a lame one. "You'll leave when your year is over, then." This was a possibility she hadn't even considered. But wouldn't that be easier than watching him with Doreena?

"No," he said, straightening. "We're no longer engaged. Well, she may be engaged, just not to me."

"Oh, Adam, I'm so sorry." She took a step toward him, then stopped. She didn't trust herself any closer.

"I've been surprised to discover that I'm not. Sorry, I mean. It's a blow to my pride, I suppose, but it's also a relief."

Part of her wanted to rejoice at his words. Ingrained caution wouldn't let her. "That's terrible, Adam."

He laughed. "Yeah, I know. Sit down." He indicated the blankets on the floor. "I need to talk to you about Peggy, but first let me tell you about Doreena and me."

Jane couldn't help the suspicions that clamored in her brain. "Sit down? Here?"

"Those chairs aren't very comfortable, and I don't have a porch swing."

"Porch swing?"

"Please, Jane." He sat cross-legged on the blanket. When he stretched his hand toward her, she threw caution to the wind.

Chapter Nine

Adam had to tell her why she wasn't getting Peggy. But not yet. First she had to understand that he cared about her. And before he could tell her that, he had to explain about Doreena.

Jane had seemed so carefree when she sat on the blanket to be near Peggy. Now she sat primly, her hands folded in her lap, her back straight. She seemed hesitant, self-conscious. She was also farther away. Adam wanted to move toward her, but knew she scared easily.

"Doreena and I met shortly after her father had taken an interest in me," he began. He watched her closely as he went on. "But I should go back farther than that. I was raised in an orphanage."

Her eyes widened, and he knew he had her compassion. That wasn't what he wanted. "The orphanage was one of Mr. Fitzgibbon's favorite charities. Every year or so he would pick out a boy who was doing particularly well in school and give him a boost toward higher education.''

"And you were his choice," Jane guessed. "That was very kind of him."

"Yes, it was," Adam agreed. "Fitzgibbon believed one should make his own fortune so his help didn't include much in the way of monetary assistance. His recommendation helped me get into medical school, but I had to find a way to finance it myself."

"Which is where Clyde came in." Her hands were resting demurely in her lap, and Adam wanted to take one into his own. She seemed so distant, isolated. But what could he expect?

"Fitzgibbon threw a large party to introduce me and make sure the story made the papers. It was at this party that I met Doreena. She was unlike any girl I had ever seen."

Adam had to laugh at himself. "That sounds funny now. How many girls did I know? There wasn't much socializing at the orphanage. I had worked in a neighborhood store since I was fourteen so I wasn't completely sheltered, but I wasn't prepared for Doreena.

"I don't know what she saw in me. Maybe the rich are fascinated by the poor. The reverse is definitely true. Her house, her clothes, her...style had me in awe.

"Through two years of medical school, we saw each other nearly every week. She would usually initiate it. I had had to leave the orphanage when I was eighteen, and Fitzgibbon had arranged for me to live at a boardinghouse for young men that was located near the college and housed primarily students. I paid for my rent by washing dishes.

"There was a common room downstairs where we could entertain guests. Or in Doreena's case, she would entertain us. She loved to play the piano and sing or show off her paintings. All the boys were in love with her."

Looking back, Adam could see how much she'd enjoyed the attention. He had been her ticket into the gathering of young, adoring men. But he hadn't seen it then. He had watched her captivate the others and had felt only pride.

"When I was about to graduate, I asked her to marry me. Her parents strongly discouraged it."

Jane was watching him with sad eyes. "What did they say?"

"Doreena didn't tell me everything they said, but I understand 'disown' came up at least once. They were convinced I was after her money."

Jane wasn't looking at him now, and her face was hard to read. He had talked too long about Doreena, anyway. "The point is," he added, "I don't think she would have agreed to marry me if her parents hadn't objected. It was an act of defiance, but I didn't see that at the time.

"Ever since I got here, I've been trying to imagine Doreena in this house. I've been trying to figure

out what she was going to find to do here. I don't
think she would ever have been happy.''

"You were never in love with her,'' Jane said.

Adam wasn't sure if it was a question or an ac-
cusation. He could only answer honestly. ''I thought
I was. But no, I don't think so now.''

"You would think a person would know—about
love, I mean.''

Adam understood that while his confessions
might let Jane know that Doreena was no longer
between them, they didn't really cast him in a very
good light. ''You'd think so, wouldn't you? Maybe
I let myself be fooled. Or maybe we did love each
other, just not enough to give up anything else we
wanted.''

"Is that what love is?'' Her voice was very soft
and made him think of Peggy's whispers. ''Giving
up something?''

"I don't know. It just seemed to come down to
that.''

"I don't think Grams believed in love.'' Jane
shook her head. ''I know she loved me and she
loved my mother, but I don't think she believed that
men knew how to love.''

"That's silly, Jane. We're not that different.''

Jane was quiet for a moment, gazing down at her
lap. She looked so vulnerable, so nearly frightened,
that he wanted to comfort her. He wanted very much
to take her into his arms. He realized he had wanted

to many times before, but hadn't allowed himself to admit it because of Doreena.

But what would Jane think if he did, if he moved a little closer and put his arm around her shoulder? That this was all a calculated seduction? Especially considering what her grandmother had told her. He forced himself to be satisfied with capturing one of her hands between his.

"Why would your grandmother believe that, Jane?"

Jane shrugged, unwilling to look at him. Still, she didn't pull her hand away. "I don't know anything about my grandfather. Grams never mentioned him. I can only assume he disappointed her, somehow. Maybe he left her.

"My mother ran away with my father when she was very young. He dragged her all over the country. When I was born she didn't want to travel anymore, but he wouldn't change. I think he was a gambler, I'm not sure. My mother took me and moved back to live with Grams. Grams was poor but she made room for us.

"I was only seven when my mother died, so I don't really know what happened, but I remember her fighting with Grams. I think she thought my father would come after her, but Grams was right. He never did."

When she didn't go on, Adam spoke softly. "My mother left me on a doorstep. I don't mistrust all women because of it."

Jane turned to him then, her eyes startled. "How could she do that?"

Adam laughed. "She was probably hungry. But I didn't mean to interrupt you. How did you and your grandmother get out here?"

"We got a letter from George Pinter saying that my father had died. He owned a house here in Clyde, which now belonged to me. Evidently there was a will and papers that included our address, even though he never wrote to us in all those years.

"Grams sold what she could, abandoned the rest, and we took a train out here. The house, by the way, was this one. But Grams fell in love with the house next door. When its owners put it up for sale, she made a deal with the bank. We've been paying off the loan with money from the boarders."

"And that's why you work so hard." He moved closer, barely conscious that he was doing so.

"Partly," she said.

He couldn't resist reaching out to touch her face. Her skin was soft and warm. She smelled of lilac soap and cinnamon, a delightful combination he had only encountered in Jane. He slid his thumb slowly across her lips. They opened with a tiny gasp that made them all the more tempting.

"Jane…"

He looked into her eyes and forgot what he had intended to say. Their dark depths were filled with longing. Longing that he was sure matched his own. Very slowly, wanting to draw out every moment, he brought his lips to hers. They were softer than he could have imagined.

He savored their sweetness for a long moment, then slowly drew away. "I want you, Jane," he whispered.

Somewhere in the back of his mind he realized that wasn't what he should say. There was something else. Something important.

But what could be more important than holding Jane? Her hands were resting lightly on his ribs, and he could feel her trembling. He didn't want her to be afraid. He tried to wrap his arms around her, but, sitting as they were, it was a little awkward. He brought his lips to hers again and lowered her gently to the floor.

The confusion Jane felt when Adam first leaned toward her was quickly replaced with something she had no name for. She had been aware of her attraction to Adam for some time, had fought the desire to be near him, to hear his voice, to savor the slightest accidental touch.

She wasn't fighting now. She knew she should be. But this was the first thing that had felt right in a long time. And he was so gentle, achingly gentle. She found her hands grasping the fabric of his shirt.

"Shh," he whispered, making her realize that she had moaned aloud. "I want to show you how I feel. I don't know how to tell you. Let me show you."

His lips hovered above hers as he spoke, then settled over them again, eliciting another moan. This kiss was stronger, more demanding, driving the last objections from her mind.

His fingers alternated between stroking her burning skin and unfastening her buttons. She was much more aware of the former than the latter. Each touch produced a desire to touch him as well.

He rose above her to balance on his knees. She was afraid it was over, that he had had enough. She followed him up, ready to plead for one more kiss. Before she could speak his lips found her willing mouth, and she read an urgency she had missed before. It spoke to something deep inside her.

She was more ready than ever to plead with him to stay when she heard a collar button skitter across the wood floor. She took that as a good sign and helped him with the buttons on his shirt. It was soon tossed aside, followed by an undershirt, leaving a broad expanse of bare chest and lean ribs for Jane's eager touch.

While she explored the texture of taut flesh and the sprinkling of fine hair, he went to work on the bodice of her dress. Though he had hurried with his own shirt, he seemed to take an excruciating amount of time with hers. With each button he teased the skin beneath it or dipped his fingers under the lace of her chemise. By the time he pulled the hem free of the waistband of her skirt, she was breathless.

How odd that she didn't feel embarrassed, sitting before him in her undergarments. He didn't seem to be disappointed, but rather looked at her most admiringly.

Had he seen Doreena like this? Did Jane really want to know if he had?

His eyes locked with hers and all other thoughts fled. She felt his warm fingers trail down her throat and slip slowly beneath her chemise. His eyes never left hers, watching, perhaps, for her reaction.

She had no thought of stopping him, even when his hand encircled a breast and gently lifted it free of the lace barrier. She had had no idea how sensitive her skin could be, how exciting it was to feel her nipple harden under his palm.

She couldn't stand the intensity of his eyes any longer and closed hers. At once she felt dizzy, as if she were floating, then realized he had lowered her back to the floor.

While her fingers twined in his hair, he spread kisses on all her newly exposed skin, sending ripples of sensations through her entire body. It was these sensations, she was sure, that prevented her from realizing what his hands were doing until she felt his fingers against bare skin on her upper thigh. Her skirt was bunched at her waist and her pantalets were on their way to her knees. Well, more likely her ankles.

This was exactly what her grandmother had warned her against. This was the seduction that would ruin her.

Even as the thought came she shut it out. This

was Adam. This was the man she loved. He had said he wanted to show her how he felt. She wanted to show him, too. With the slightest shift of her hips she helped the pantalets on their way.

He raised his head and looked down into her eyes as if he were surprised at the decision she had just made. "Ah, Jane," he murmured. "Tell me you want this."

A gentle tug at her knee separated her legs, and he moved to kneel between them. She felt both frightened and frustrated. She was breathing too hard to answer him.

"Tell me," he persisted. "Tell me I'm not taking advantage of you. Tell me you want this as much as I do."

"Adam," she moaned.

He leaned over her, planting a tender kiss on her lips. "Please, tell me."

"I want this," she breathed. "I want to love you."

He sealed her declaration with a fiery kiss that sent her senses spinning. By the time she recovered enough to realize he had pulled away, he had his pants nearly undone.

The lamp on the desk cast his face in a warm, soft light and left the rest of his body in shadow. Jane got only a glimpse of his manhood before he was braced above her again.

"Do you trust me, Jane?" he whispered between kisses.

"Yes," she whispered back, and marveled that it was true.

"I don't want to hurt you. Tell me if I hurt you."

This was a new aspect she hadn't considered. She tensed, but his kisses quickly banished any thought of pain from her mind. Desire that had seemed to tingle in every part of her body began to center itself between her legs, causing her to arch toward the warm body that pressed against her.

Perhaps he sensed her urgency because the next moment he let his member brush against her, then slowly eased inside of her. The sensation was too exquisite. Jane moaned, but what passed her lips was Adam's name.

"Jane," he breathed.

With one swift movement, he entered her, tearing the barrier and making her cry out at the sharp, unexpected pain.

"I'm sorry," he soothed near her ear. "Please, forgive me. I didn't want to hurt you. It'll pass soon."

He kissed her cheek, and she knew he was kissing away her tears. He was right, though—already the pain was fading and the earlier desire was returning full force.

He murmured against her cheek, "I'll stop if you want, Jane."

"No," she whispered, clinging to him. She found it impossible to keep from moving against him, under him, around him. They were one. The realization filled her with awe.

In a moment, all thought was overshadowed by the feelings that built inside her. His breathing quickened to match hers and she realized he was feeling the same things she was. She clung to him and called his name as they went over the brink together.

The world seemed to hang suspended for several minutes. Jane came back to the present when Adam rolled off her. Her clothes were a tangle around her. She started to sit up to bring them somewhat aright when he caught her and brought her up against his side. "Don't go anywhere just yet."

She snuggled against him, content to do nothing more.

"I can't believe we did that," he murmured.

"Regrets already?" she asked, feeling a pain much sharper than she had felt moments earlier.

"Not regrets, Jane," he said. "I just want you to know I didn't plan this."

"Neither did I," she said, feeling a little defensive, but uncertain why.

"I know." He found her hand and twined his fingers with hers. "I only meant to talk to you. But it'll keep until morning."

Morning, she thought, *after a night spent in his arms.* She couldn't possibly sleep like this. But moments after she thought it, she found herself drifting off to sleep.

* * *

Adam shook Jane out of a deep sleep. "It'll be light soon," he said softly.

"What?" Jane started to push herself off her bed to see who was in her room, then realized she wasn't in her room. A naked Adam was lying on his back looking up at her with a seductive smile on his face. She quickly adjusted her chemise to cover herself more effectively.

"Much as I hate to let you go, you probably should get back to the boardinghouse."

"Yes." She tried to shake the sleep out of her brain.

"We'll be along later for breakfast."

"We?"

He grinned at her then, evidently enjoying her confusion. "Peggy and I."

"Peggy!" Only yesterday Jane had vowed to work twice as hard to prove to the placing board that she could support Peggy. Here she was in Adam's front room, her clothes in shambles and her brain too foggy to think of anything except the man beside her. She had to get away from him so she could think. "Yes, bring her over for breakfast."

She found her bodice and slipped it on, her fingers shaking as she worked the tiny buttons. Her pantalets had also been tossed aside but she was too mortified to do anything but wad them up and clutch them to her side.

To make matters worse, Adam had come to his feet and fastened his pants as if it didn't bother him

at all to do so in front of her. She started for the
door, but he caught her arm. "Better use the back
door," he said.

She turned toward his kitchen, but he didn't let
her go. He drew her into his arms instead and
planted a slow, devastating kiss on her lips. By the
time he was through she had to rely on him to point
her in the right direction. She looked back once to
see him watching her with what could only be described as a satisfied grin on his face.

She hurried across the dark yards and crept into
her kitchen. She went from elated to mortified and
back at least three times before she closed the
kitchen door behind her. What had gotten into her?
At the same time she wondered how she could have
resisted. In truth she had wanted this to happen, had
dreamed of it, for weeks.

Oh, Grams would have been so upset with her!
In all her twenty-two years she had never seriously
questioned anything her grandmother had told her.
Until now.

How could what had happened between her and
Adam be so terribly wrong? Adam wasn't like her
father or her grandfather. He wasn't going to aban-
don the woman he loved.

But hadn't he loved Doreena until recently?

Jane tried to shove the thought aside. Doreena
was different, she told herself. Doreena didn't want
to be part of Adam's life. She had rejected his love.

And he had sought solace in someone else's arms.

Not liking the way her thoughts kept turning, Jane decided to put Adam out of her mind, at least as much as possible. She had the dishes from last night's buffet to clear away, then she would prepare a special breakfast. She wanted everything to be perfect. George and Adam, too, would realize that she could provide for a little child.

But first, she needed to run to her bedroom and change into a fresh dress, not to mention pantalets.

Adam stood smiling long after Jane left his house. What a treasure he had almost missed. What if Doreena had married him when he'd asked her to? What he had felt for her could hardly be compared to what he felt for Jane.

Maybe fate had played a hand. Or maybe Doreena was more perceptive than he was. Either way, he felt as if he had just missed stepping off a cliff.

With a light heart he gathered up his scattered clothes, found all but one of his collar buttons and folded Jane's blankets. He noticed she had left the tray sitting on his desk. He could return it when he went for breakfast. There was no evidence that Jane had shared the meal with him.

The blankets could raise a few eyebrows, however. Besides, he might need them tonight. With any luck, he would again be sharing them with Jane.

Once his front room was tidy, he went to the kitchen to warm some water to shave. When he was finished, he went quietly up the stairs. He hadn't heard a sound from that direction and assumed Peggy was still sleeping.

At first he thought the little girl was hidden under the tangle of blankets. As he approached the bed, however, he realized that it was empty.

"Peggy?" Adam called softly.

The room was quiet.

"Oh, please, be up here somewhere," he muttered. He knew she liked to hide. He hoped to God she didn't like to run away. Might as well start with the obvious. He tossed the covers that were dragging on the floor back onto the bed and looked underneath. Nothing but a little dust.

None of the other furniture in the bedroom left space either under or behind for a little child to hide. Adam covered the area thoroughly and sprinted down the stairs. The image of the little girl wandering around town in the dark, half-dressed, spurred him to search faster. He headed for his desk next, thinking she might have returned there while he and Jane were sleeping. His search of that room and his examination room proved fruitless.

All that was left was the kitchen, and he had been in there only a few minutes before. Still, he hadn't been looking for a little girl.

He was reviewing possible hiding places as he entered the room, and went straight to the pantry. There he found Peggy, curled up on the floor, his chunk of cheese wrapped in her arm like a doll. His tin of crackers sat open at her knees.

"How often in your life have you been fed, little one?" he whispered. He knelt beside her and eased the cheese out of her grasp. He wrapped it back in its cloth and set it on a shelf, noting a few telltale tooth marks.

Peggy awoke when he put the lid back on the cracker tin. She seemed frightened for a second, then simply curious. "You hide, but you're not afraid of me," he said.

She didn't answer.

"I'm glad you're not afraid of me. Did you get hungry in the night?"

He didn't expect an answer and didn't get one.

"Let's go upstairs and get dressed. We get to go have breakfast with Jane. You like her, don't you?" He stood as he spoke and lifted Peggy under her arms. Half a dozen crackers scattered onto the floor. They had evidently been rolled in her petticoats.

Peggy watched them with alarm. Adam, once Peggy was balanced on his hip, reached down and retrieved one of the crackers. "I don't see how one more can ruin your breakfast," he said as Peggy took the cracker.

She didn't eat it, though, just held it firmly in her hand as he helped her into a clean dress and ran a comb through her fine brown hair. He sat her on the bed and put her shoes on her swinging feet.

"Can you sit right here while I put on a clean shirt?"

Peggy just looked at him.

"If I keep talking to you, will you stay put?"

She swung her feet against the side of the bed, making a rhythmic thumping sound.

"That's good. Just keep that up." He was fighting with his collar when the thumping stopped. He spun around to face the bed and watched Peggy slide to the floor. She walked carefully across the room, her leather-soled shoes making almost no sound on the wood floor. She headed for the chair that held her suitcase. Adam watched as she tugged at the little apron that Jane had laid across the opened lid.

The apron fell to the floor at Peggy's feet. Adam worked another button through the collar as he watched her try to put the apron on. She might have managed it but for the cracker.

"Want some help?"

She glanced at him but continued to try to pull the apron over her head with one hand. Adam knelt behind her and helped her finish, tying the bow at her waist. As he stood, he saw her slip the cracker into the pocket.

Or what was left of the cracker. There were quite a few crumbs sprinkling the floor at her feet.

"Now I know why you like the apron," he said, turning to find his necktie. He turned back a moment later and she was gone. "Peggy?"

How could she move so fast and so quietly? Surely she hadn't had time to go downstairs. He scanned the room and almost missed her. She was crouched on the floor under a window, half-hidden by a bookshelf.

He decided to leave her. If he tried to coax her out, she'd just find another place to hide. He finished getting dressed, glancing often toward the little girl. Finally he joined her in the corner.

"Are you hiding from me?"

She stared at him.

He smiled and got a smile in return. "Let me show you something," he said, moving from her to the window. He turned the latch and raised the casement. "Come help me guess what Jane's fixed for breakfast. Smell that? Bacon, I think. Biscuits? What else?"

Peggy moved toward him, evidently smelling the food, too.

"Shall we go see?"

If he hadn't caught her, she would have tried to go out the window. "Let's take the stairs, all right?"

Downstairs, he remembered the tray. He wondered how he was going to carry the tray and keep ahold of Peggy. As soon as he set her down, she headed for the kitchen. He grabbed the tray and followed. Once he had turned the doorknob for her, Peggy headed straight for Jane's kitchen door.

Chapter Ten

Jane must have heard Peggy rattling the door because she opened it before Adam had caught up with the little girl. Peggy took in Jane's warm greeting and stepped across the threshold. Jane opened the door a little wider to admit Adam.

"I forgot all about that," she said, taking the tray.

"Now why would you do that?" he murmured.

She turned her back to dispose of the tray, but not before he saw two pink spots brighten her cheeks. He would have loved to pursue the subject further, but Peggy had disappeared.

"Peggy?"

"She went in the dining room," Jane said, obviously unconcerned.

"She's probably stuffing her pocket full of scrambled eggs," he said as he went after her.

Peggy had climbed up on a chair and was eyeing the array of food with wonder. As far as Adam could tell, she hadn't touched anything yet.

"Let's go wait in the parlor," he said as he lifted her out of the chair.

She grabbed a biscuit before he got her clear.

"On second thought, let's keep the crumbs in the dining room." He carried her around the table and sat her next to his usual place. She munched contentedly on the biscuit.

Jane came in with a bowl of spiced applesauce. "Will you tell the others it's ready?"

Adam nodded. "Watch her. She's a slippery one."

"I know her tricks," Jane said with a smile.

Adam found the others in the parlor and directed them to the dining room.

"How's that little girl this morning?" George asked.

"Fine," he answered. "It was just a case of stage fright yesterday."

"Glad to hear it." George ruffled the child's hair as he went by. "Then we should start looking for a family right away."

"So this is one of the urchins," Nedra said, taking her place across from the child. "She needs to learn some manners."

Adam looked down at Peggy. Other than a few crumbs in her lap and one or two on her chin, he saw nothing wrong with the way she was eating.

"Little girl," Nedra said, "put that on your plate until the rest of us are seated."

Peggy went still.

"Leave her alone, Nedra," George said.

"Well, one can't start too soon with their training. Right, Naomi?"

Naomi seemed to sense that the men in the room weren't in agreement and chose them over her sister. "Well, she isn't really our business."

Once Jane had taken her seat, Adam slid into the chair beside Peggy. The little girl was still staring at Nedra. "Go ahead and eat, Peggy," he said softly.

She continued to stare at the yellow-haired woman across the table. Peggy was so short Adam guessed she only saw the woman's head.

"Well," Nedra said, staring back. "She's certainly a strange creature, isn't she?"

Adam was sure Peggy thought the same of her.

Jane started the platters around. She had prepared quite a feast. He wanted to suggest that she was spoiling them but didn't want her blushing in front of the group. He'd tease her later.

In spite of the variety of food, he couldn't interest Peggy in anything but staring at Nedra. The first time the woman bent over her plate, he discovered why Peggy had watched her so closely. The little girl slid out of her chair, walked almost soundlessly across the room and slipped behind a curtain.

Adam was sure everybody at the table saw her go, with the exception of Nedra. The woman was visibly startled when she glanced up and saw the empty chair.

"Even I would put a stop to that," Naomi said.

"Where did she go?" asked her sister.

Naomi pointed.

"Well!"

George broke the tension at the table with a laugh. "You know, I'd hide, too, if Nedra glared at me."

Nedra turned and did just that.

George laughed again.

"She's afraid of crowds," Jane said. "Let her hide until we've finished. She can eat later."

Nedra and Naomi seemed pleased with that suggestion. They turned the conversation in another direction, toward young Ferris, as a matter of fact. Adam watched Jane as she kept an eye on Peggy.

Ferris and Bickford had left the house and the Cartland sisters were on their way up to their rooms when George mentioned the orphan again.

"I'll put the word out that the little girl's available," he said, rising from the table. "That is, unless you want to change your vote, Adam."

Adam froze. He knew he should have told Jane last night. He watched the color drain from her face.

George showed no remorse for the revelation as he walked past them. It was clear to Adam that George wanted Jane to have the little girl, perhaps to save him the trouble of hunting up another family. But George took all of Jane's labors for granted. He didn't see that she worked herself to the point of exhaustion.

"Jane," Adam began, "I can explain."

"You don't need to explain. You've already told me you don't think I'm competent to run this boardinghouse. Of course I wouldn't be able to care for a child besides."

"Jane—"

"When were you going to tell me?"

"I meant to last night but I...we got distracted."

Her mouth fell open in shock. For a moment he thought she might slap him.

"What *was* last night?" she asked softly. "Consolation? Or am I supposed to be so overwhelmed with gratitude that I would forgive you?"

Adam had a feeling he was missing something here, something important. "Gratitude?"

"Yes," she said, scooting back her chair with such force it screeched against the floorboards. "That you would even consider me after the perfect Doreena."

"Oh Jane, don't accuse me—"

She stood. "Let Peggy eat whatever she wants. I'll clean up after you've gone."

"Jane." He came to his feet, but she was out of the room before he could stop her. Her bedroom door closed with a definite snap, if not the slam he was expecting.

He slumped back into his chair. Why hadn't he had the sense to explain to her last night? He knew why. His common sense had deserted him entirely the first moment he'd touched her. What were the chances she'd believe that now?

A tiny sound reminded him he had other responsibilities. He moved to the corner and crouched down, pulling the curtain aside. Peggy stood against the window, tears running silently down her face.

"Don't cry," he said, lifting her in his arms. "Did we scare you? It's all right." He carried her to the table. With her napkin he gently wiped away her tears. She sniffed once but seemed to be through crying.

He filled a plate for her with a little from each of the platters. "Nobody's mad at you. Old Adam here's the one who messed up."

Peggy got up on her knees so she could reach the food more easily. She did a surprising job of putting away a good portion without ever touching the spoon or fork. Adam was glad she hadn't stayed to eat with the Cartlands.

"What now, Peggy? Do you want anything else?"

Peggy licked off three of her fingers and pointed.

"Applesauce? Just don't try to put it in your pocket." He brought the bowl nearer and dipped some onto her plate. "How about trying the spoon this time?"

Peggy dipped her fingers in the sauce as Adam scooped some onto the spoon. "Here, you can get more this way."

Peggy let him bring the spoonful to her mouth, then nodded at this new way to eat. After licking her fingers, she opened her mouth for more.

"You hold the spoon," Adam suggested, putting it in her sticky palm.

She was a little awkward, but it worked better than her fingers. When she had scraped up all the sauce and licked the spoon clear up the handle, she looked over the table again.

"What next?"

Peggy chose a biscuit, and Adam wasn't at all surprised to see her try to shove it into her pocket. "That may not be a bad idea," he said, helping her break the biscuit until it fit. "I'm not sure we'll be welcome here at dinner."

He wiped her hands with the napkin and decided that wasn't going to do it. "Let's go wash up."

He helped her out of the chair and took her hand. Peggy continued to lick off the other while she let Adam lead her to the kitchen.

The smells of Jane's kitchen made Adam think of her. He wanted to go knock on her door and see if she would listen to him. But what would he do with Peggy? Once the child's hands and face were clean he stood her on the floor and looked down at her. She craned her neck to look up at him.

"Maybe if I clean up from breakfast she'll forgive me. What do you think?"

Peggy stared.

"I think it's worth a try. Why don't you hide under Aunt Jane's kitchen table while I wash her dishes? Does that sound fun?"

Peggy didn't move.

"Here." He moved to crouch beside the table. "You can crawl under here and pretend...whatever it is you pretend."

He was a little surprised when she came forward, bent down more than was necessary and sat on the floor beneath the table.

"Good. Now stay there, please, and don't hide anywhere else."

Adam made a quick trip to the dining room for plates, checking, as soon as he returned, to be sure Peggy hadn't disappeared. She sat right where he had left her, whispering to herself.

He was well into the china when he heard the front door open and someone call for Dr. Hart. He moved into the dining room, rolling down his sleeves as he went. "In here," he said.

An elderly woman came cautiously into the room. "Are you Dr. Hart?"

"Yes, ma'am. What can I do for you?"

"I brought my husband in to see you. Shall I bring him in here?"

"Next door. I'll be with you in a second." He turned quickly back to the kitchen and tossed on his suit coat. "Come on, Peggy. We have to go."

He was relieved to see that Peggy hadn't moved. He knelt down and lifted her out from under the table. "You can hide under my desk for a while. All right?"

She didn't seem to be alarmed at their abrupt departure. The old couple were waiting in his front room when he arrived. He let Peggy down and watched her walk across the room and slip around the desk.

The couple watched her, too. They both gave Adam a questioning look. "Peggy, from the orphan train," he said.

They nodded in understanding. "The one that got sick," the woman said. "We hear she's touched in the head."

"Now that's not nice, Margaret."

"I didn't say anything against her. I just said what I've heard."

Adam cleared his throat. "She's, ah, a little unusual, I'll have to admit. What can I do for you?"

The man spoke. "You can pull this tooth out so I can think about something else."

Jane heard the woman call for Adam and decided she had sat in her room and felt sorry for herself long enough. Berating herself for being a fool didn't help her get her work done. She had a kitchen to clean and some shopping to do. And then another meal to prepare.

She would like nothing more than to tell Adam he wasn't welcome at her table, but he was a paying customer. She needed the boardinghouse more than ever now. She had to prove that she could make the place work, pay off her debt and own the house free and clear. She had to prove it to Adam and to herself.

When she knew Adam had left, she came out of her bedroom, prepared to face the mess in the dining room. She tried to tell herself that she was surprised that Adam had started the dishes. But she wasn't surprised at all. He would have finished them if he hadn't been called away.

Why couldn't he be as wonderful as he seemed?

It wasn't entirely the fact that he had denied her a chance to have Peggy, though that hurt, of course. What broke her heart was the fact that he had taken advantage of her grief last night. He had made her think he loved her, though this morning she couldn't remember him ever saying that he did.

She continued to berate herself as she tackled the rest of the dishes. In spite of all her grandmother's warnings, she had made the same mistake her mother had. She had trusted a man with her heart.

It wouldn't help to mope around. Her garden had been neglected while she cleaned the house. There was always plenty to keep her busy.

By the time she was setting the table for dinner that evening she wondered if she would ever be so busy that she didn't think about Adam or Peggy or the two of them together.

While she was picking fall peas, she had seen them leave the house. She had been sweeping the front porch when they returned. She hadn't meant to check the clock or wonder why they had been gone for three hours. She didn't need to know where they had been.

She shouldn't be curious whether Peggy had said anything aloud to Adam. If Adam was growing attached to her or was eager to see her off with some other family.

They weren't, either one of them, a part of her life except as paying guests at her table. Her life was the boardinghouse and that's all it would ever be. She wasn't making the same mistake again.

She plucked an ant off the chrysanthemums in the center of the table and went back to the kitchen to check on her pork chops. She was coming back into the dining room when Peggy entered from the other direction.

She heard Adam call after her, "Peggy. We should wait—"

He stopped when he saw her. Jane had frozen at the sound of his voice. Disappointment, anger and longing all washed over her as if she hadn't spent the day trying to prepare herself for this meeting.

She didn't want to react this way. She wanted to think he was no different to her than George or Mr. Bickford. The best she could do was pretend. And the easiest way to do that was turn her attention to Peggy. The little girl stood still between the two adults, perhaps sensing the tension.

"Good evening," Jane said. She put the platter of chops she carried in its place on the table and knelt down beside Peggy. "Did you and Dr. Hart have a good day?"

Peggy gave her a shy smile.

Jane tried again, whispering this time. "What did you do today?"

"Puppy," Peggy whispered.

"You saw a puppy?" She hadn't meant to look up at Adam. She certainly hadn't meant to smile.

"I had to make a house call," he said. He was still standing just inside the room as if he were afraid to come any closer. *Good,* she thought. She wouldn't be able to think if he was any closer.

"Did you ask for one?"

He shook his head. "They were kind of big for Peggy. She was a little overwhelmed."

Jane bent toward Peggy's ear. "Were they big puppies?"

"Big," she whispered back.

Jane stood, taking the child's hand as she did so. "Adam, any time you want to leave her with me, you know I'd love to have her." She shouldn't have said it aloud. Not to Adam. It made her way too vulnerable.

"I know, Jane," he said softly.

Jane heard her front door open and George's voice. "Would you tell the others dinner's ready?" she asked, turning away. "Peggy can help me get the last of it on."

In the kitchen, Jane looked around for something Peggy could carry. All that was left was a bowl of turnips, not a good choice for little hands. She considered letting Peggy carry the serving spoon, but she might be tempted to lick it. Peggy settled instead on an extra napkin. "Can you carry this to the table, sweetheart?"

Jane brought the turnips to the table as the others were taking their places. Peggy dropped the napkin and made a beeline for the curtains.

Adam intercepted her. "How about eating with the rest of us?"

Peggy didn't seem to mind being carried to the table, but she didn't want to sit in her own chair. Adam settled for letting her sit on his lap. The Cartland sisters looked askance at the arrangement, while Bickford and young Ferris simply seemed uncomfortable.

George, on the other hand, seemed delighted. "How did our doctor fare today with a little tagalong?" he asked as the platters were started around the table.

Adam's laugh sounded a little self-conscious. "We got along. Peggy liked riding the horse. Didn't you, Peggy?"

Peggy hid her face in Adam's jacket. Adam smoothed a lock of baby-fine hair behind the child's ear. "I imagine she's pretty tired."

Jane felt a stab of jealousy. She wanted to be the one Peggy turned to for comfort. She wanted to hold her and rock her to sleep. And that wasn't all of it. She knew what Adam's fingers would feel like against her cheek, and she wanted that, too.

She was so caught up in her own mix of emotions she almost missed what George was saying. When he mentioned Peggy, he had her full attention. "The husband said he'd bring his wife into town to meet her on Saturday."

Saturday! That was only three days away. Jane had thought she'd given up any idea of changing the board members' minds. She'd thought she had adjusted to the notion of never having Peggy as her own. In that moment she realized she had not. As long as Peggy was at Adam's there was a chance. After Saturday her chance would be gone.

Jane couldn't eat. She couldn't even pretend to eat. She tried not to watch Peggy fall asleep on Adam's lap. She didn't want to think about either of them at all. But what else was there to think about?

She looked around at the people who shared her table. The Cartlands flirted with Ferris and Adam and the unresponsive Mr. Bickford. They talked about a dress shop they would never open. Bickford spent his summers writing a novel he would never finish. And she dreamed of a family she'd never have.

How long before Ferris settled into his job and quit thinking of anything higher? What had George's dreams been before he settled for bachelorhood and a small-town bank?

And Adam? Was he still dreaming of Doreena? They were a pretty sad lot, the bunch of them, she decided. A shy, whispering orphan fit right in.

* * *

Adam wanted to put Peggy down to sleep in the parlor, and stay and help Jane with the dishes. He needed to talk to her, whether she wanted to listen or not. But Peggy cried when he stood up, though she tried not to make a sound. She clung to him, whispering something in her silent sobs. She seemed to be in the midst of some bad dream. He took her home and held her until she was sleeping soundly again.

Jane had offered to send some dinner home in case Peggy woke up hungry in the night. He had assured her that Peggy had eaten all afternoon. Now he wished he had told Jane to bring it over in an hour. Maybe he could have trapped her in his front room and made her listen.

He touched Peggy's cheek to reassure himself that she was all right. He was afraid the nightmares might return, and even if they didn't, he didn't like the idea of her wandering around his house in the dark. He decided to sleep beside her on the bed, or at least to try. He didn't expect to get Jane off his mind.

Early the next morning, he was awakened by a pounding on his door. He threw on his shirt, tucking it into his pants as he ran down the stairs. He opened his door to find a haggard looking man on his doorstep. In the gray morning light, Adam could see horror in the man's eyes.

"My boy," the man said in a choked voice. "You gotta hurry. My boy shot him."

Adam decided not to try to make sense of what the man was saying at the moment. "Go to the livery and tell Knapp to saddle a horse for me," he said. "I'll be right out."

Adam closed the door as the man hurried toward his waiting horse. What to do about Peggy? He could wake Jane, but he hated to; she had looked exhausted at dinner last night.

He had checked his bag to be sure he had everything he needed, and was dressed to leave and still hadn't made up his mind. He gathered Peggy into his arms and carried her down the stairs.

Outside, the man was waiting with the horses. He didn't seem surprised to see a little girl, or perhaps he was too dazed to fully comprehend it. Adam passed Peggy to the man while he mounted. She stirred when he took her back into his arms, then clung to him. He decided it was probably better that he was taking her. Jane didn't need to worry about a distraught child while she tried to fix breakfast.

On the way, the man tried again to explain what had happened. As Adam understood it, Mr. Norse and his son had gone out before dawn to see what was disturbing their chickens. They had lost several during the past few days and suspected a raccoon. They were determined to kill the thief this morning.

He had thought his younger son was safe in the house. It hadn't occurred to him or his older son that the boy would want in on the excitement. It had been dark. The older boy had seen something move.

Adam's first treatment of a gunshot wound in the Wild West was going to be on a seven-year-old boy.

A boy of a dozen years or so met them as they rode into the yard. He held the horses without a word. His pale face and haunted eyes told Adam he was the one who had shot his brother.

Norse dismounted and took Peggy as he had before. This time the little girl slept through the transfer. "Ma'll make a bed for her," the man said. "Little Nick's in our bed and the boys are in the loft. Can't have her fallin' from there."

The man and his wife had enough to worry about without being bothered with Peggy. Adam wished he had left her with Jane. It was too late for that now, though, and he followed the man into his house.

Mrs. Norse came from behind a curtain. Upon seeing Peggy, she gathered blankets and made a bed for her in a corner near the door. From the muted conversation between husband and wife, Adam guessed they had heard all about the strange little orphan girl.

Leaving her in their care, Adam pushed aside the curtain and turned up the lamp. The boy lay still on the bed, his breathing slow and even. Adam carefully removed the bloody bandages that covered his right side. Bleeding had slowed enough that Adam could at once determine several individual injuries. Nick had taken the very edge of a shotgun blast. His brother, fortunately, had nearly missed him.

When the parents joined him he asked for warm water and lots of clean cloth. He would have to remove the shot. He took the necessary implements from his bag as he waited for the couple to return. With the curtain drawn, he could see Peggy sleeping in the next room. He prayed that both children would sleep through the surgery.

With the parents nearby to keep little Nick still, Adam began probing for pieces of shot. He glanced up once to see Peggy sitting on the pallet, watching them. He hoped she didn't become frightened. At that moment, he couldn't think of any good reason for not having left her with Jane.

She was still sitting quietly the next time he looked, and he worried less about her. Nick and his parents seemed to be holding up admirably well. Adam hadn't seen the older boy since he had taken the horses, and determined to speak to him before he left.

He was nearly finished when he glanced up to find the blankets empty. Peggy had wandered off, probably looking for food or for a place to hide. He shouldn't have been surprised; he had been working for what would have seemed like a terribly long time to the child. Surely she would be safe, and they could find her later. He tried to concentrate on finding the last pieces of shot, but a part of him still worried about Peggy.

He stitched up the torn flesh and instructed the

mother on dressing the wounds. "Let me fix you some breakfast," she said once he was finished.

"I'd appreciate that," he answered. Maybe the smell of food would bring Peggy out of hiding.

He stepped out the front door and, finding the older boy sitting on the step, sat down beside him. "Your brother's going to be fine," he said.

"I shot him. I'm never picking up a gun again."

Adam nodded. "That's probably not too bad an idea. You're a lousy shot, anyway."

The boy's laugh sounded almost like a sob.

"Did you see a little girl come out here? She seems to have wandered off."

"Yeah," the boy said. "She was following one of the kittens."

"I better go try to find her."

The boy, who gave his name as Rick, helped him search the barn and the other outbuildings. They had exhausted all the obvious places when his mother called them in for breakfast. Rick seemed to be more worried than Adam when they returned to the house.

"Followed a kitten, did she?" asked the father when they told him of the missing girl. "Then it should be easy to find her."

Adam and Rick exchanged a glance. "I guess it's your turn, then, Pa," Rick said.

The man laughed and went back into the house.

"Bet he's already found her in there," Rick mumbled.

They started to follow him in, only to watch him

leave again carrying a bowl of milk. On the front porch the man called, "Kitty-kitty-kitty."

Half a dozen kittens came from all directions, and hot on the trail of a yellow-and-white one came one little girl. "Peggy's! Peggy's!" she called.

It was the first time Adam had heard her speak aloud.

When the kitten stopped at the bowl of milk, Peggy scooped it up and held it. "Not too tight, sweetheart," Adam said, coming to the kitten's rescue. "Hold little kittens very gently."

Peggy's hold loosened slightly, and she cuddled the kitten, rocking a little on her tiny bare feet.

"Let the kitten eat its breakfast," he said, taking the animal out of her arms. "You're hungry, too, aren't you?"

Peggy let the kitten go and let Adam lead her away, but she watched the kittens over her shoulder all the way into the house. Once at the table, she took a slice of bread in one hand and a piece of bacon in the other and slipped back off the chair.

"Please, stay here," Adam said, lifting her up again.

Peggy sat obediently for about a minute, then slipped off the chair once more, using the other side this time so she was out of Adam's easy reach.

"We don't take offense at her manners," Mrs. Norse said. "Let her watch the cats while she eats."

Adam kept an eye on the portion of the porch he could see through the open doorway, afraid Peggy would follow the kitten again. After a couple of minutes of standing, she sat down. As long as Adam could see a bit of her dress and apron, he knew she was still there.

"Will she want some more?" Mrs. Norse asked.

"I think she'd be back if she was hungry," he said, picturing Peggy putting bacon in her pocket.

She sent Rick out with another slice of bread, anyway. He returned without it, and Adam decided that was at least better than bacon.

Adam checked on Nick while his brother saddled his horse. When Adam stepped out onto the porch, he found Peggy sitting just where she had been, with the white-and-yellow kitten curled up in her lap. She looked up at him and smiled.

"Whatcha got there, Peggy?" he asked, crouching down beside her. "Can you say kitty?"

"Nonny," she said. "Peggy's Nonny."

"Sweetheart, I'm afraid that's Nick's Nonny, I mean kitty."

Mr. Norse had followed him out. "Nick likes the black one, don't he, Ma?"

Rick, waiting with the horse, was the one who spoke in agreement.

"I'd be obliged if we could take the kitten," Adam said. "This is the first she's spoken out loud and hasn't wanted to hide someplace."

"Well, I swear," the man muttered. "Reckon you oughtta take a couple?"

"No, thanks," Adam said, coming to his feet. "I think this one will be just perfect."

Chapter Eleven

Adam and Peggy got back into town about midday. As they walked from the livery to the house, Peggy carried her kitten and whispered to it. Adam thought he ought to carry her, since he had been in too big a hurry that morning to put on her shoes. He watched the little girl walk across the uneven ground as if she were more used to going without shoes than wearing them.

When they came to the boardinghouse, Peggy turned up the walk. "Peggy," Adam said, waiting at the street.

She ignored him completely. With the kitten in one hand she tried to turn the doorknob. She switched hands and tried again. Adam walked up the steps behind her.

Peggy's little fist pounded on the door. "Ann Jane," she called.

Jane threw open the door. "Did I hear you *calling* me?" Her eyes met Adam's. "Did you hear that?"

"There's more," he said.

"Peggy." Jane knelt down in front of the little girl. "What have you got?"

"Nonny." She held the kitten out proudly.

"Nonny's beautiful," Jane said, stroking the yellow-and-white fur. "We missed you at breakfast."

She was talking to Peggy, but Adam decided to answer, anyway. "We were called out to a patient."

"Was it serious?" She kept one hand on Peggy's shoulder as she stood.

"Serious enough."

"You should have left Peggy with me."

"I know. But we wouldn't have gotten the kitten if she hadn't come along." She returned his smile; a good sign, he hoped.

"Are you hungry?" she asked.

Adam shook his head. "I think I'll see if Peggy will take a nap. We'll be back for dinner."

He hesitated just a moment, trying to think of a reason to stay a few more minutes. Peggy yawned noisily, as she had several times on their ride back into town. "We better go," he said.

Jane nodded. She bent to give Peggy a kiss and the kitten one last stroke. She whispered something in Peggy's ear that made the little girl nod.

Adam took Peggy's free hand and led her away.

Jane watched them go. She was sure it had been Peggy's idea to show her the kitten. She felt flattered.

She wasn't sure how she would feel if she thought

Adam had suggested it. Her feelings for Adam were completely confused. She didn't trust him, should never have trusted him, but she was afraid she still loved him.

Jane thought Adam looked a little haggard when he arrived for dinner. She wasn't sure whether to be pleased or not. If he had enough difficulties, he might be willing to let her have Peggy. On the other hand, he might be even less inclined to believe that she could handle the child.

Peggy had avoided the parlor and its occupants and headed straight for the dining room. Adam had been right behind her.

"Did you have a good nap?" Jane asked the little girl.

Adam answered for her. "The kitten slept. I had patients all afternoon, and I guess they kept Peggy awake. Can we talk after dinner?"

Jane hoped her trepidation didn't show when she agreed. She turned her attention to Peggy. "Let's go find something for Nonny's dinner. He can wait in the kitchen while we eat."

Peggy followed Jane into the kitchen. So did Adam. Jane tried to ignore the latter. She poured some cream into a saucer and set it on the floor. Peggy put the kitten down and sat beside it. The kitten purred as it lapped up its dinner. Peggy looked up at Jane and smiled.

"Let's go get our dinner," Jane said, reaching a hand toward the girl.

Peggy shook her head.

"Come on, Peggy," Adam said. "You didn't have much at noon. You've got to be starving."

Peggy shook her head again.

"But Aunt Jane's dining room smells so good," he coaxed. "Let's go see what she made."

Peggy bit a finger, as if torn, then pointed to the kitten. "Nonny, too."

"Nonny can wait right here." Adam lifted Peggy to her feet.

When he took her hand, she pulled away. "No."

Adam looked taken aback. Jane couldn't suppress a smile. "At least she's talking."

He scowled at her, and she bit her lip. Crouching down beside the little girl, she said softly, "Nonny will wait for you, Peggy. As soon as you've both eaten, you'll be together again. Look how hungry he is. Aren't you hungry, too?"

Peggy's brow furrowed. "Peggy's Nonny," she declared.

"I know. I'm not taking him. I'm just feeding him. Kittens can't come to the table. The Cartlands would faint." She turned Peggy's face toward hers and smiled. "That would scare your little kitty, wouldn't it? He better hide in here."

Instead of the smile she had hoped to get, Peggy's face crumpled completely. "Nonny say hide," she cried, as tears spilled from her eyes.

Jane drew the girl into her arms. She looked up at Adam for help but he shrugged. "Your kitten wants you to hide with him?" she asked. That would make some sense. Peggy didn't like eating with the others, anyway.

"Nonny say be kayet."

"What, sweetheart? Your kitten wants us to be quiet?"

Peggy cried softly against her shoulder.

Adam had knelt down beside them. He ran a comforting hand over Peggy's back. "I think she's too tired to understand that we're not taking her kitten."

"Maybe we should let her wait in here," Jane suggested.

Adam sighed. "That would be easiest, but is it a good idea in the long run?"

Jane shook her head. "I don't know. You're the guardian."

His eyes locked with hers and narrowed slightly. She wondered what he was thinking. That she would take the decision off his hands if he would change his vote? Of course she would.

Finally he spoke. "Peggy, do you want to wait in here?"

Peggy drew away from Jane. "Nonny gone," she said mournfully.

"Nonny's right here, sweetheart."

"Nonny gone," she repeated. She sat down on the floor and snatched the kitten away from the cream. Nonny seemed only momentarily startled by this sudden change in fortune. He settled into her lap, licking delicately at his face and paws.

Jane and Adam rose to their feet. "Let's go eat," Adam said. "She'll be all right in here."

George asked after the orphan; everyone else accepted her absence as a return to normalcy. Jane couldn't stop thinking about her, though. Halfway through the meal she went in to check on her and found her sleeping on the floor. The kitten, having finished the cream, was curled up beside her.

She reported this to Adam while the others at the table were deep in a conversation of their own. He nodded, but didn't seem pleased. She could guess what he was thinking. The child's sleeping patterns weren't fitting well with his life. Part of her hoped Peggy kept him up all night.

When the others left, Adam began stacking dishes. Jane decided to let him. It would be nice to have a little help again. She started toward the kitchen with two of the platters, but Adam stopped her.

"Let's talk before we wake Peggy."

"All right," she said, turning back. He pulled a chair away from the table and took the platters out of her hands, indicating a chair. She sat as he swung another chair around to face her.

"There are a couple of things I need you to understand," he began.

She heard her grandmother's voice in her head and determined not to believe him. But she had to listen. In spite of everything, she wanted him to say he loved her, and she wanted to believe him.

But evidently that wasn't what he had wanted to tell her.

"I'd like for you to have Peggy," he began.

Jane found herself holding her breath. Was this it? Had he finally changed his mind?

"But I'm afraid to give her to you."

Her breath left her all at once. "Afraid? What are you talking about?"

"Jane, I've seen how hard you work." He tried to take her hand but she pulled it away. "You let everyone take advantage of you."

"Including you."

He flinched at that, and she counted it a small victory. While he seemed to scan the room, searching for words, she kept her eyes locked on his face. She couldn't afford not to.

"What I'm trying to say is that I worry for your health. You're not sleeping."

He reached out to touch her face, but she drew back. She didn't want him noticing anything about her that was less than perfect. She especially resented him pointing out the very things she noticed every time she looked in the mirror.

"You're already beyond your limits," he continued. "A little girl, especially this little girl, would be too much for you."

Jane had to fight for calm. He made her feel defensive, more vulnerable than ever. She wished

Peggy would wake up and interrupt, put an end to the whole conversation. "Who are you," she said finally, "to decide that for me?"

"I'm a doctor," he said easily, "and I'm on the placing board. I have to think of what's best for Peggy.

"But, Jane," he added, moving closer, "I'm thinking of you, too. I can't watch you work yourself into an early grave because you're trying to prove something to your grandmother."

She felt tears sting her eyes and tried to blink them away. "You know I don't own this house. You know I have to have the boarders and the guests at dinner or I'll lose it. Are you asking me to choose between Peggy and my home?"

"I'm not asking you to do anything. I just want you to understand why I voted the way I did and why I can't change it."

She struggled to hide the full extent of the pain she was feeling. He knew way too much already. Like a flash of light, realization dawned. "You still want the house." He shook his head to deny it, but she pressed on. "You think if you have this house, you can win Doreena back."

He started to speak, but she wouldn't listen. "That's blackmail, Adam," she declared, coming to her feet.

"Blackmail? Jane, I don't want to take your home. I certainly don't want Doreena."

She had started toward the kitchen with some idea

of waking Peggy and sending both of them out of her house when he caught her arm and spun her around to face him. "Jane, I love you."

She silenced the part of her that wanted to believe him, and managed to speak softly, though she wanted to scream. "You'd say anything, wouldn't you?"

He was startled enough to drop her arm. She turned and walked with as much dignity as possible toward the front hall. This last lie had cut too deep and tears were already running down her cheeks.

"You're hiding," he said. "You're hiding just like Peggy does."

He'd followed her! She hadn't anticipated that. She hurried to her room and slammed the door, certain he wouldn't breach it, though why she trusted him at all she didn't know.

"Damn it, Jane, you're twisting everything I say."

He was right outside her door. She stuck her fingers in her ears so she wouldn't have to listen to him, but gave it up to cover her mouth instead. She didn't want him to hear her crying.

"Jane, please, listen to me."

Her head flew up at the sound of his voice, no longer muffled by the door.

"Oh, Jane."

He moved to sit beside her on the bed, and wrapped her in his arms. She wanted to resist but found it impossible. His gentle hands cradled her head against his strong shoulder. "All I seem to do is make girls cry," he murmured.

Jane sniffed, trying to control her tears. She didn't like her broken heart being compared to Peggy's tantrum, but she couldn't think of any scathing retort.

"How can I prove I love you?" he whispered.

She could guess what he considered proof. The last thing she wanted him to know was that she longed for that "proof" every night.

"Keep Peggy tomorrow," he said suddenly.

She drew away. "What?"

"Keep her tomorrow. See how you get along."

Jane waited. What was the price? When he added nothing more she said, "Let her sleep here tonight."

He shook his head, and she added quickly, "She's already asleep. I have an extra bed right off the kitchen. Besides," she noted, surprised that she could find a smile, "you look like you could use a good night's sleep."

"I can't sleep for thinking of you." He brushed a tear off her cheek.

She sprang to her feet, stepping out of reach. "Come help me tuck her in."

When the two of them were fussing over the sleeping child, Jane decided that had been one of her dumbest suggestions. It reminded her too much of Peggy's first night at Adam's. *Her* night at Adam's.

Peggy slept through the process. The kitten didn't,

however. It explored the kitchen and the adjoining room, climbed the blankets to the bed and jumped to the floor again.

Jane watched the kitten and found herself smiling. "Do you want to take Nonny?"

"And risk Peggy waking up to find her kitten gone? I wouldn't do that to you, honey." The endearment came so easily from his lips she wondered if he even noticed. He was, after all, teasing.

"Let's get to those dishes," he added.

She should send him away, tell him she could wash the dishes much more quietly alone. She couldn't bring herself to do it.

When the dishes were nearly finished, an intermittent clattering caught their attention. The kitten had found something behind the cupboard that he batted this way and that. Adam went to investigate and retrieved a collar button.

"How did that get there?" Jane asked.

"I'm a master at losing them," he said, dropping it into his pocket. The kitten watched the prize disappear, then scampered off after some invisible foe.

Jane tried to remember when Adam had actually removed his collar and got a sudden flash of finding him in her dining room the morning after Grams had died. For days afterward there had been things out of place that the Cartlands claimed no knowledge of. Adam had cleaned up after their breakfast.

That didn't really surprise her now, though it would have then. But it did make it clear that he had done it with no expectation of reward. She would never have known if not for the collar button.

Adam stayed until the last dish was put away, and still seemed reluctant to go. Jane couldn't think of a good excuse to ask him to stay, and wondered why she wanted to. He evidently couldn't think of anything, either, and said good-night.

Jane checked on Peggy and found her sleeping soundly. The kitten had finally settled down at the foot of the bed. In her own bedroom, Jane left the door open a crack so she would hear Peggy, certain the child would wake up hungry before morning.

She thought of the packet of letters she had found among her mother's things, but decided not to read them tonight. She was certain she was already tired enough to sleep.

Johnny eased open the door of the toolshed to look out at the train station across the tracks. It was almost dark. He had taken refuge here earlier in the afternoon when he had run from the boxcar that had brought him into town. He had twice checked the letters on the train station with the ones on the paper the cowboy had given him. He was sure this was Clyde, Kansas, the place where they had sent his little sister.

When he had first jumped aboard a westbound train he had no idea how far he would have to go. Once during the journey, he had looked out the door of the boxcar at nothing but grass and had realized if the railroad men caught him and forced him off the train, he would starve to death in almost no time. But he would probably go crazy even sooner.

At least here in Clyde there were a few houses, though they were short and crude and spaced too far apart like his friend Spike's teeth. But houses meant people and people meant food. He was more than ready to let his nose lead him to somebody's kitchen.

He eased the shed door open a crack more and slipped his narrow frame outside. Keeping in the shadows as much as possible, he set out to explore the town. If you walked too far in one direction you found yourself in that ocean of grass. He was really in the middle of nowhere. Besides that, there were no people out and about, though lights burned in several windows.

He had had plenty of time to think while he waited for dark. Unfortunately, he hadn't figured out how he was going to find his sister. She could have been hauled out of town to some farm or other. He had seen a few of those isolated cabins from the train. Peggy must be terrified. And so was he every time he considered the possibility of never seeing her again.

Maybe he'd think better when his stomach quit growling. He was following some very pleasant smells. He hoped the houses would be easy to break into. The last thing he needed, now, was to be arrested.

The house he settled on was a large one for this little town. There were lights from some upstairs windows, but the lower level was dark. He circled to the back and discovered a faint glow in some windows there. He approached with more caution. Peeking though a window he discovered an empty kitchen with a lamp left burning on the table. Someone must be expected home. This could be tricky. Perhaps he should choose another house.

His stomach rumbled, forcing the decision. He'd pick a place to hide first thing and be on the lookout for this late arrival. He withdrew the pick from the seam of his shirt and prepared to unlock the door. The knob turned easily in his hand. They had left the door unlocked! What easy pickings this town might turn out to be.

Inside, he latched the door and scanned the room. An opened door suggested a pantry, and he moved silently toward it. He froze in the doorway when something moved in the darkness. A moment later, a kitten flitted past his feet, making him gasp before he caught himself.

He had taken another step into the room when some instinct told him the cat wasn't its only occupant. He eased back, ready to run.

"Nonny?"

Could he have imagined a voice so clear? "Peggy?" he whispered.

"Nonny!" Before he could clamp a hand over her mouth, she had shouted it.

"Peggy," he whispered fiercely, his hunger forgotten. He had found her! But what was she doing here, sleeping just off the kitchen? Was she the family's maid? She was just a baby!

He heard a sound from deeper in the house. "Come on, Peggy, we have to get outta here!"

He tried to pull his sister toward the door, but she resisted, straining toward the kitten. "Come on," he whispered again.

A door opened and a woman came through it. "It's all right, sweetheart," she was saying.

Johnny froze at the back door, one hand on the knob and the other holding Peggy's. The woman froze, too, looking frightened at first, then simply curious. "What are you doing here?" she asked. "What do you want with Peggy?"

Johnny tugged on Peggy's arm, still hoping to run, but she pulled away. He didn't want to leave her but he couldn't help her from a jail cell. He flung open the door and started out into the night.

"Nonny!" Peggy shrieked.

He paused, uncertain for a moment, then turned back into the house. The woman didn't look cross or mean, but he knew he couldn't trust her. He didn't close the door behind him.

Peggy threw herself against him, clinging to him. He wrapped his arms around her and eyed the woman. "Don't worry," he murmured. "I ain't leavin' you."

The woman smiled a very pretty smile. "I know

why you look familiar," she said. "What's your name?"

He hesitated, cautious about giving out any information. Finally he muttered, "Johnny."

"Nonny," Peggy echoed imperfectly.

"She's missed you," the woman said. "How did you find her?"

Johnny shrugged.

"I'm Jane, by the way. Are you hungry? I think Peggy is. She went to sleep before dinner." Jane moved toward the cupboard. They had another chance to run. Johnny tugged on his sister's hand, but the effort was only halfhearted. He was starving and Jane promised food.

She was setting plates at the kitchen table when a man stepped into the open doorway right behind Johnny. The boy flung himself away, maneuvering Peggy behind him.

"What's going on?" Adam asked. "I heard Peggy scream and thought you might need some help. Who is this?"

"This is Peggy's brother, Johnny," Jane said.

The man's face registered surprise. He asked, as she had, "How did you find her?"

Johnny scowled. "Who are you?"

Adam stuck out a hand. "Dr. Hart, Jane's neighbor."

Johnny eyed the hand a moment before taking it briefly. Peggy slipped away and climbed up in a chair to watch Jane. "Food, Nonny," she informed him. "Good food."

Johnny watched Jane butter a slice of bread and hand it to his little sister, who took it, smiling up at the woman.

"Come sit down, Johnny," Jane said. "You can tell us how you found your sister and how you were separated in the first place. Adam, could you bring in a couple more chairs?"

While the man she called Adam was gone, Johnny walked cautiously to the table and sat across from his sister. He would eat, at least, then look for an opportunity to escape. Adam returned with the chairs and positioned one for Jane next to Peggy. He turned his own around to straddle it. The adults gave each other a curious glance before turning to stare at Johnny.

Johnny considered his situation while he helped himself to bread and cheese and cold roast beef. If this was how they usually fed Peggy it was no wonder she trusted them. Perhaps if he told them how he had found his sister, they would let him take her and go.

"Well," he began around a mouthful of beef, "when Peggy first disappeared, I asked around. Spike, that's my friend, said he heard that two men and a woman took Peggy away. I figured they put her in one of them orphan asylums. I broke into four of them at night but couldn't find my sister."

He spread a slice of fresh bread with butter.

"Next, I started hidin' on the playgrounds 'til they let the kids out. Finally, I found a boy what remembered her bein' there. He said she'd been sent out west.

"I marched right up to the prison guard, or whatever they call themselves, and demanded they send my sister back." Johnny couldn't help puffing out his chest a little and smiled at Peggy's giggle.

He glanced at the adults, who seemed to be watching in shocked silence. Pleased, Johnny continued, "The guard said he didn't know where they sent her, just that she was turned over to this society. He gave me their address, then tried to get me to go to some shelter. I lit out before he could catch me.

"Spike helped me steal some clothes and a fake mustache from a theater. You shoulda seen me, Peggy, I looked real elegant."

"Elegant," she mimicked. He gave her a wink.

"I found the place and said I was her uncle." He decided not to mention that the man in the office hadn't believed him. "I demanded to know where they'd shipped my niece. He looked up in his file and told me Clyde, Kansas."

Johnny piled more of the beef on another slice of bread and gave the adults a moment to digest what he had told them so far. They didn't need to know that he had thought Clyde, Kansas, was a person rather than a place or that he had nearly tripped on his way out because the stolen shoes were too big.

"How did you manage to find your way here?" the man called Adam asked.

Johnny chewed and swallowed. "I jumped a train that was heading west. After a couple of days, I was discovered and had to run. I met up with a cowboy who told me what I needed to know to get here."

"What did you plan to do once you found your sister?" Adam asked.

Johnny shrugged. "I'll take her back where we belong."

"And you belong in an alley somewhere?"

"We don't belong here, that's for damn sure."

"Damn sure," mimicked Peggy.

Johnny grinned. The woman chewed on her lip like she didn't want to laugh and the man was trying not to show his annoyance, and failing.

"And why is that?" Adam asked.

"There ain't nothin' here!" Johnny declared, surprised at the question. "There's just some houses in the middle of nothin'."

"And there are endless opportunities for you in the city?"

Johnny grinned at Adam. "For me there are." He rubbed the tips of his fingers together.

"As a thief," Adam provided.

Johnny tried to stare the man down, but his eyes didn't waver. Finally Johnny looked down at his plate.

Adam asked softly, "And your sister, what are her opportunities?"

Johnny looked at Peggy. She had eaten her fill
and was dropping crumbs on the floor for her kitten.
He imagined looking after the little girl in the streets
of a city. He had tried and had lost her. He had
thought he had left her in a safe place, as if anywhere on the streets was truly safe. He had been
only a few blocks away when a constable had seen
him snatch an apple from a cart. He had to run. By
the time he had been sure it was safe to return, his
sister was gone.

"Johnny," Adam said into the silence. "I'm impressed that you could track your sister all the way
out here—"

Johnny interrupted with a return of his old bra-
vado. "He's *damned* impressed, ain't he, Peggy?"

"Damn pressed," chimed the girl.

Johnny tossed Adam a defiant grin.

"But," Adam continued, doing a better job this
time of hiding his irritation, "your choices now are
to find yourself a life out here, or go back alone."

Johnny narrowed his eyes at the man's challenge.
Before he could respond, however, the woman said,
"You don't have to decide anything now. You're
welcome to stay here as long as you like."

She rose from her chair and brushed his hair off
his brow. He surprised himself by not flinching
away from her. He knew what she was thinking; his
hair was just like Peggy's.

"Johnny," Adam said, coming to his feet. "Why

don't you spend the night at my house? I'll help you get cleaned up before breakfast.''

This time Johnny did flinch. ''You think I'm dirty?''

''I know you're dirty.'' Adam waved the boy toward the door.

''Baths ain't good for you,'' he protested, but he stood, too, taking a tentative step toward the door. It was usually better to obey adults, or at least pretend to.

''Trust me. A bath would be good for you.''

Johnny hung his head and shuffled toward the door. Peggy climbed off her chair and ran after him.

Something passed between the man and the woman. It was almost as if the woman was pleading with the man, but Johnny didn't understand.

The man seemed to, however. He crouched down and took Peggy by the shoulders. ''Aunt Jane wants you to stay with her tonight. Johnny's going to go to my house for a bath.''

''Go, too,'' Peggy said.

''We'll be back for breakfast.''

''Peggy's Nonny,'' she insisted, grabbing Johnny's hand. He held on tightly, not wanting to be separated, either.

What the woman said next was more bewildering than all the rest of the strange events of the evening. ''Flip you for them,'' she quipped.

Chapter Twelve

Adam wasn't sure he should have given in. Peggy and Johnny were both sleeping in the bed off Jane's kitchen. If he knew Jane at all, she'd be washing the sheets in the morning.

Adam's biggest concern was that Johnny might try to take his sister and run. He had threatened the boy with jail for breaking into Jane's house if he tried. They'd be easy to find, Adam had told him, here in the middle of nowhere.

He had further insisted that Johnny come to his house early in the morning, before his sister woke up, if possible, and get that bath. The boy seemed to prefer that to the possibility of Jane giving him one. Adam was fully prepared to go get Johnny if he didn't come of his own accord.

Meanwhile, he lay in bed and thought of the turn things had taken this evening. After what Johnny had gone through to find his sister, it would be cruel to separate them, but he wasn't going to make it any easier to place the girl. It did, however, explain some of her strange habits.

Jane, on the other hand, wasn't any less likely to want her. In fact, Jane's inclination to protect children would probably have her volunteering to take Johnny as well. The amount of trouble that boy could get into was easy to imagine.

The next morning, Adam found Johnny waiting in his kitchen. Waiting didn't quite describe it. Lurking did. Adam had the distinct impression the boy had been going through the cupboards and drawers and had only stopped when he heard Adam coming.

The boy himself confirmed it. "If'n I'd picked your house last night, I'da starved."

"I eat most of my meals at Jane's boarding-house." Adam lit a lamp and went to light the stove. "Pump that pan full of water and we'll heat it for your bath."

"Is that why Peggy's there—Jane's boardin' her?"

Adam wasn't sure how much he ought to explain to the boy. "She was left in my care," he said, "but Jane wanted to keep her last night."

"She tryin' her out to see if she likes havin' a girl?"

Adam lifted the pan onto the stove to heat. "She knows she likes having a little girl, we're just not sure she can take care of her and run the boarding-house at the same time."

Adam handed the boy a bucket. "Fill this," he said.

"You already decided you don't want no little girl?"

Adam brought the tub inside before he answered. "I've already discovered it's hard to make house calls and keep her safe."

"Then neither one o' you's gonna mind when I take her with me."

Adam lifted the full bucket out from under the spout and poured it into the tub. He handed it back to Johnny, who turned to fill it again.

"Johnny," Adam said after a moment, "I volunteered to help find families for a group of orphans. I'm not going to just forget about one of them."

Johnny spun around. "Well, we ain't no orphans. Whatcha think about that!"

Adam looked at him a moment. "You're runaways?"

"We're throwaways. But it ain't none of your business. Anyhow, *Peggy* ain't no orphan 'cause she's got me. And I ain't leavin' her."

Adam let it go. Showing him what his sister's life could be like out here was going to make more of an impression, anyway.

Half an hour later he had Johnny dressed in clean clothes with rolled-up cuffs and a cinched-in waist. Johnny declared that he looked funny.

"That was the whole reason for giving you a bath," Adam said.

Johnny nodded as if he believed it, but his eyes held the grin he would have denied. "I hope Peggy's awake causin' trouble 'cause I'm gone."

"Well, I hope not, but it's time we went to see."

They found Peggy on her knees on a kitchen chair, sipping from a coffee cup.

"They feedin' you coffee already?" Johnny asked.

Peggy scrambled off the chair to meet him. Before she flung herself into Johnny's arms, Adam noticed that her face bore traces of recent tears.

"She thought she had dreamed you," Jane said, turning from the stove.

"Bet you were hopin' that's all I was," Johnny said.

Adam wanted to cuff his ear for talking to Jane that way, but she just smiled. "You're not quite the nightmare you think you are."

"I'd reserve judgment," Adam said.

Johnny shot him a wicked grin, then knelt down to give his sister his full attention. "Look at you! You got shoes. Where'd you get them shoes, baby?"

Peggy brought a leather-clad foot down on the wood floor and laughed at the sharp sound. The kitten ran up to pounce on her foot.

"You reckon I can borrow 'em sometime?"

Peggy shook her head. "Peggy's shoes." She bent and picked up her kitten.

"Breakfast will be ready soon," Jane said. "Do

you want to wait in the dining room, or in the parlor with the others?''

Before Adam could protest, Johnny spoke up. ''I think we should wait in the parlor, don't you, Dr. Hart?''

There was obvious challenge in the boy's tone. ''The parlor it is,'' Adam said.

''Can the kitty stay here and have its breakfast?'' Jane asked. Peggy relinquished the kitten and took her brother's hand.

Adam led the way to the parlor, where the Cartlands already waited. Both women looked surprised when the children entered.

''Nedra and Naomi Cartland,'' Adam said. ''This is Peggy's brother, Johnny,''

''He's not wearing shoes,'' remarked Naomi.

''And you ain't wearin' no corset,'' Johnny said.

''Johnny!'' Adam's sharp command was nearly drowned out by the women's gasps of outrage.

Johnny looked up at Adam. If he was trying for innocence, he was failing. ''Go sit down,'' Adam said, indicating an unoccupied settee.

Johnny helped his sister into the chair and sat down beside her. Adam took a seat nearby, ready to stop him from moving but uncertain how he would stop him from talking.

Ferris joined them, followed almost immediately by George.

''Who's this?'' George asked.

Adam explained briefly about the boy's arrival.

"There were several farmers wanting a boy,"
George said.

Adam heard Johnny's intake of breath and put a
hand on his shoulder, hoping to forestall an outburst.
"I think we better try to keep them together," he
said.

George nodded. "I suppose you're right, considering. We don't want them running off."

Adam's hand on his shoulder wasn't enough to
stop Johnny this time. "Why the hell not?" the boy
asked. "What difference does it make to you? Do
you own her or something?"

George wasn't as surprised at the outburst as the
others. "I was thinking of your health and safety,
son," he said. "As well as your sister's."

"Why don't you save yourself some trouble and
just not?"

"Johnny," Adam asked quietly, "do you want
breakfast?"

Johnny cast him a rebellious glare he took to be
a yes. "Then you treat everyone in this house with
respect."

Johnny settled back into the cushioned seat. "It
ain't right," he muttered. "You put me on a farm,
I ain't stayin'."

George looked like he was enjoying the whole
situation. "What's Jane think about the boy?" he
asked.

"I don't know, but I can guess," Adam said. Jane

would want them both. She would think she could love the boy into angelhood.

Jane called them in for breakfast before Johnny treated them to his opinion on Jane. When they were seated around the table, Peggy and Johnny separating Adam from Jane, Bickford joined them. He gave the boy a glance and then a shrug. He evidently figured two urchins were not much different than one.

When Nedra glared at Peggy for eating with her fingers, the little girl waited for a chance to slip out of her chair.

"Where ya goin', Peggy?" Johnny asked.

The girl pointed to the curtains. "Hide."

"You don't need to hide no more. I'm here."

Peggy turned around and with Johnny's help climbed back into her chair. He tried to encourage Peggy to use her fork but he wasn't doing a whole lot better himself. He seemed as overwhelmed by the amount of food as Peggy had her first time.

"You always eat like this?" he asked Jane as the others were finishing up.

"No," she said, smiling. "I fixed a little extra because I thought you might be hungry."

The boy seemed taken aback by this news.

"Do you still want to keep Peggy today?" Adam asked when the others had left the table.

"Sure. She can play in the yard while I garden, and help me bake a cake for dinner. I'm sure Peggy wants you to stay, too, Johnny."

Adam guessed the boy misinterpreted that to mean Jane *didn't* want him. Maybe he'd be on his best behavior if he thought she would send him away. Though exactly what Johnny's best behavior might be, he didn't know.

"You can stay," he said, "if you help with the garden."

"Gonna have me farmin' one way or another, ain't ya?"

Adam ignored him. "But first, we're going to help with dishes."

Jane wanted to laugh at the way Adam and Johnny squared off. Adam was sure the boy was going to cause her trouble. She was just as sure he wasn't.

He was bound to cause Adam trouble, however. Adam watched him so closely while they dried the dishes that she was surprised either one of them got anything done.

Peggy wanted to help, too. Jane moved a chair for the little girl to stand on so she could wash. Peggy poured water from one cup to another until all the rest of the dishes were done. All in all, the chore took longer than it might have, but it was fun having her kitchen full of voices.

Especially Adam's. She didn't know what to think about him, what to trust, what to believe. But this morning, with the children around her and his warm voice instructing Johnny, she decided not to think, just enjoy.

After he left, giving Peggy a hug and Johnny a pat on the back, Jane tied an old coat button to a string and gave it to Peggy to tempt her kitten with. Johnny helped Jane dig potatoes and weed the garden. These were not skills he had any experience with, but he caught on quickly enough.

He watched Peggy, too, she noticed. When she followed the kitten around to the front of the house, he called her back.

"Nonny lost," she said, pointing in the direction the kitten had gone. "Nonny find."

"You ain't callin' me the same name as that cat," he said, putting aside his hoe and going to her. "You gotta learn to say Johnny. J-J-Johnny."

"J-J-Nonny," she said.

Jane could see him shake his head, but he must have been smiling because Peggy giggled. The kitten scampered into the yard, and Peggy was after him again.

Johnny came reluctantly back to the garden. "Ain't we killed enough weeds yet?"

"Do you want to help me wash some sheets?"

"What do you think?"

Jane laughed. "Poor Johnny. This must seem awfully strange to you. How would you like to go shopping? We might find clothes that fit you better and order some shoes."

"You don't need to do that," he said, giving her a wicked grin. "I can lift anything I want."

"I'm sure you can, but I'd rather you didn't. Folks around here are liable to recognize their clothes if they see you wearing them."

He cocked his head to one side and gave her a quizzical look. "How come you ain't shocked?"

She smiled as she gathered the hoe and bucket of potatoes and walked back toward the house. "Maybe because you're trying so hard to shock me. I suppose if I had to live the way you have, I'd steal, too. But you're not on your own anymore. There are people who want to help you."

He called his sister, then followed Jane into the house. "You think that Dr. Hart wants to help me?"

"Yes, I do."

"I think he wants to send me to jail."

Jane laughed. "What makes you think that?" She poured water into a basin and washed Peggy's face and hands.

"I think it 'cause he said it."

"That's called a threat," Jane said. "He wants you to behave and stay out of trouble." She washed her own face, then motioned Johnny to take his turn.

"You mean he won't really do it?"

"He'd rather you heed his threat and be good," she said, "But he might do it, all right."

He tossed her a grin. "Is that a threat, too?"

"Don't push your luck," she said, tousling his hair.

Jane counted out some of her small hoard of money. She could buy a few things for Johnny without running short on the payment to the bank. Though it would mean skimping on a few things for herself, she was happy to do it.

Their first stop was Chinnock's, where Johnny's feet were measured for shoes. They visited several other stores, but Jane couldn't interest Johnny in any of the clothes.

"I'll get my own back," he assured her.

The fact that his own were practically rags evidently hadn't occurred to him. "I plan to feed you so well that they'll be too small," she said instead.

His response was a shrug.

Peggy, with the kitten in her arms, seemed fascinated by all the merchandise in the stores and was content to simply gaze around her at each stop.

Jane bought what she needed for dinner and let Johnny carry part of it home. While Jane put things away, Johnny went outside to watch Peggy. When Jane joined them she found them on her porch eating smashed versions of the bread she had served at breakfast. Evidently they hadn't expected to be fed again anytime soon.

"How about another slice of bread," Jane suggested, "with some ham on it this time?"

Johnny tried to hide his surprise. "That'd be all right."

Peggy was already used to being fed on a regular basis and dropped the crumbling bread for her kitten. "More," she said, coming to her feet and following Jane into the kitchen. She climbed into a chair to watch Jane make the sandwiches.

"Do you like mustard?" Jane asked.

Peggy stared.

Jane took Peggy's hand and put a drop of mustard on one of her fingers. Peggy licked her finger and made a terrible face. "Like," she said.

Jane laughed. "You like it?"

"Nonny, too," Peggy said.

"Which Nonny? Nonny Kitty or Nonny Johnny?"

"Nonny Nonny," she said.

Jane put a little mustard on four sandwiches. She wrapped them in a cloth and put them in a basket along with three cups and a jar of milk. She helped Peggy out of the chair. "Let's have a picnic," she said.

Peggy ran to her brother. "Picnic," she announced.

Adam tried to ignore the noise coming from next door. It was a little early to go to dinner. Still, the children were his responsibility and perhaps he should see what the ruckus was about.

As he crossed from his backyard to Jane's, he could see sheets flapping on the line, along with several dresses that looked suspiciously like the Cartlands'. Running under and around the sheets and dangerously close to the garden were at least a dozen children. Maybe not quite a dozen. It was hard to get a reliable count, since they were all moving.

The kitten snoozed, well out of harm's way, beside the back door. Adam sat down on the back step and murmured, "How can you sleep through that?"

"That ain't fair!" Johnny called. "You always catch Peggy 'cause she's little."

"Nonny it!" squealed Peggy, trotting up to him and smacking him on the back.

"Yeah, all right. I'll be it. Now, you run away."

It was pretty clear Johnny had picked out whom he planned to tag. The boy was probably close to the same age but nearly twice Johnny's size. "You ain't been it yet, Riley," he said as he stalked more than chased the other boy.

"You ain't been it 'til now, neither."

"That's 'cause I'm good, not 'cause I hide behind my sister."

"I don't hide behind my sister," Riley protested, circling around a tall girl Adam now recognized as Rosemary Finley.

"You're gonna get me caught again, Riley," Rosemary shouted, trying to avoid both boys.

"Save me, Rosemary," Riley cried, laughing, "or I'll tell Ma you were playing tag with the boys."

A couple of girls left the pack of shouting participants. Suzy Gibbons and Peggy walked hand in hand toward the house. "I think she's tired," Suzy said, collapsing in the grass at Adam's feet. Peggy climbed up on his lap, sighing heavily.

"Does your mother know you're here?" Adam asked Suzy.

She nodded, unconcerned. "I have a kitten but it's bigger than Nonny."

"Peggy's Nonny."

"Yes, I know it's Peggy's Nonny," Suzy said in a voice usually reserved for infants.

Riley made a break and headed down the street at a dead run, Johnny on his heels.

"Out of bounds!" screamed Riley's sister. She rounded up the smaller children and herded them back into the yard. "Hey, Doc," she called, seeing him for the first time.

"Hello, Rosemary."

"Johnny'll be back in a minute. He'll tag my brother when he stops to open the door." She organized another game, and Suzy ran to join.

"Do you want to play, too?" Adam asked Peggy.

She shook her head and snuggled up against him. It made him think of keeping her, of sharing a family with Jane. But he had done everything wrong, and Jane didn't trust him. He had made love to her when he should have talked to her, and told her he loved her when he should have been asking her for-giveness.

Johnny sauntered back into the yard looking pleased with himself. Adam hoped Riley was none the worse for wear. He rose to meet the boy, planning to question him, just as Jane opened the back door.

"Hi," she said, looking happier than he had ever seen her. "I didn't know you were here."

"I've been watching the children play," he said.

"Aren't they wonderful?" Jane beamed. "Help me give them their cookies, then we have to send them home for dinner."

Adam noticed she carried the cookie tin. "You're giving them cookies now, then sending them home? For dinner?"

Jane laughed. "One cookie isn't going to make any difference. They've been running around for an hour. Almost time to go," she called.

Instead of heading home, the children shouted and ran toward her. They settled down a little as they waited for her to open the tin. She handed out the cookies one by one and the children drifted away.

"Where's Riley?" she asked Rosemary, who had waited until the smaller children had all gotten their treat.

"Probably home crying."

"Oh, dear. Did he get hurt?"

"Naw, he's fine. He teased Johnny all afternoon, and Johnny chased him home."

"I did more than that," Johnny said. "I bloodied his nose."

Rosemary turned to grin at him. "Good for you. Believe me, Aunt Jane," she stated earnestly, "Riey was askin' for it. I was about ready to punch him myself.''

"Well," Jane said, obviously uncertain how to handle the situation, "take a cookie for him, anyway.''

"Oooh, sure.'' The girl grinned at Adam, making him certain the cookie would never make it home.

Adam set Peggy on her feet. She put her cookie in her pocket and sat down on the step to play with the kitten.

"Johnny.'' Adam motioned for the boy to come close.

"Nothin' doin'. If ya want to give me a beatin' ya gotta catch me first.''

Rosemary had just left the yard when she turned back. "Here comes Mama,'' she whispered. "Let me handle her.''

Rose Finley marched into view, a rolling pin in her hand. Riley was two steps behind her. A little blood crusted his face and a little more stained his shirt. He was smirking.

"That boy,'' she began before she spotted Adam. Evidently his presence made her reassess the situation. She took a less belligerent stance. "My Riley says this boy beat him up.''

Jane stepped closer to Johnny. Adam stepped up to a spot somewhere between the two boys. And the two women.

"That's right, Ma,'' Riley said. "I come over to play with the other kids and Johnny called me names, and when I tried to stand up to him, he hit me."

Rosemary ran to her brother and wrapped her arms around him in a modified hammerlock. "Poor little brother," she cooed. "That's not what happened, Mama. We were playing tag, and he fell down. He hit his nose on the ground. We would have helped him, but he ran home instead. You know how boys are. They gotta make everything sound more exciting."

Riley struggled, but she held him tighter. "Poor little brother," she said through clinched teeth.

"They're both lyin'," Johnny said.

"Lyin'," mimicked Peggy from her seat on the back step.

"Suppose you tell us what happened," Adam said.

Johnny glared at him. "Suppose you take a—"

"Johnny." Jane issued the warning quietly, but it stopped the boy.

"Well sure, I'll tell you what happened. That little toad was lordin' over all them little kids 'cause he's bigger and faster. When it looked like he weren't gonna win, he runs home. Only I'm faster'n he expected and I caught him at his door. I only punched him once. That's all I had to."

Rosemary laughed. "Oh, Mama, you know how boys are."

Rose seemed torn. "I don't see how that scrawny boy could have hurt you too bad, Riley."

"Scrawny?" Johnny started forward, but Jane's arm kept him in his place.

"I'm sorry to have bothered you, Jane." Rose smiled sweetly. "Nice to see you again, Dr. Hart."

She turned. "Let's get you cleaned up."

"But, Ma. Ow!" Riley glared at his sister.

"The idea," Rose muttered, leading her son away by the ear. "Tellin' me that boy beat you up."

Adam watched them go, then turned his attention to Johnny.

The boy gave him a wicked grin. "Now you gotta decide who you believe."

"You'd be better off if I believed Rosemary."

Johnny laughed. "Not the way I see it."

"Let's let it go for now," Jane said.

"You go on inside," Adam said. "Johnny and I'll have a little talk."

The glare Jane gave him rivaled any of Johnny's.

Adam smiled. She wasn't acting that much different than Rose. "Don't worry, I won't let him bloody my nose."

"Ain't *your* nose I'm worried about," Johnny said. "But I ain't hidin' behind no girl." He stepped away from Jane.

Jane turned and stalked off to the house. Adam heard her say something softly to Peggy before the door closed.

"Now she's mad at both of us," Adam observed.

"That bothers you more'n it bothers me."

"It ought to bother you, Johnny. She's ready to be your friend."

Johnny shrugged.

"Did you consider any way to settle your differences with Riley besides punching him in the nose?"

"Yeah," Johnny said, backing off half a step. "I considered hittin' him with a club, but I couldn't find none."

"Riley might decide to be your friend, too, if you let him."

"Now he can decide knowin' a little bit more about me."

Adam understood how impossible it would be for Johnny to admit he had made a mistake. And what had happened didn't matter as much as what might happen in the future.

"Here's the situation," he began, catching the boy's shoulder before he could dodge away. "A family is coming to meet Peggy tomorrow. I know you don't want to see her go off without you, but I also know that you aren't interested in a family for yourself. I want you to think of what this could mean for Peggy. Your smart mouth and your belligerent attitude could ruin it for her."

He steered Johnny toward the back door. "Now tell me, what's Jane fixing for dinner?"

Chapter Thirteen

Jane looked down at the children sleeping in the little bed and thought her heart would burst. She hadn't had to argue at all to get Adam to leave them another night. She was so happy she could have kissed him.

Well, she thought, feeling her cheeks grow warm, that wasn't an image she should dwell on. She dwelled on it anyway: Adam standing here beside her, watching the children sleep; Adam making love to her again. She was every bit as foolish as her mother had been.

She turned down the lamp on the kitchen table and walked quietly to her own room. She mustn't think about Adam or she would get no sleep at all. She didn't want Adam saying the children had exhausted her.

No matter how well she slept, he was taking them away after breakfast. A family was coming to see Peggy sometime tomorrow. Though Jane had suggested they could see her at the boardinghouse as easily as next door, Adam had shook his head. He probably thought she would try to keep them from taking Peggy. Maybe she would.

She told herself that Peggy deserved both a father and a mother. Perhaps the family could open their hearts to a clever boy as well. It could be the best thing for both the children. Wasn't that what she wanted?

But the answer was no. She wanted Peggy. She had fallen in love with the little girl with the strange habits, and with her brother besides. How could she not love a boy who would go to such lengths to find his little sister?

As Jane put out her lamp and crawled into bed, she told herself she must pray that whatever happened would be what was best for the children. But as she drifted off to sleep, the family she envisioned for the children included not only herself, but Adam.

When Adam was ready to leave with the children, Peggy turned back. She ran to Jane, who knelt to give her a hug and a kiss. "Ann Jane go, too?" Peggy asked.

"No, sweetheart, Aunt Jane has to stay here."

"Peggy come back."

Adam saw Jane's eyes fill with tears. "Come back anytime," she said.

Peggy, her kitten scampering at her feet, ran cheerfully back to Adam. She took his offered hand

and one of Johnny's and skipped across the back-yards to Adam's kitchen door.

Adam felt like a monster. Jane loved the little girl and would make a wonderful mother. His reasons for denying her the child were becoming less clear all the time. But now, when he would like to give in and let Jane have Peggy, there was Johnny to consider as well.

Johnny wasn't going to make anybody's life easier. The incident the evening before had made it clear the boy had his own idea of what was acceptable behavior, and there was every chance that attempts at discipline would only make him run away, perhaps taking Peggy with him.

At the same time, it seemed cruel to separate them. Adam wasn't sure he would be willing to send Peggy off with the couple today if they didn't want to take Johnny, too. He would have to try to guess whether or not they could handle the boy.

When they entered Adam's kitchen, Johnny found his old clothes and wanted to change into them. "I think you look better in those," Adam said.

"You're not serious," Johnny said, tugging at a rolled-up sleeve. "I look like an idiot."

"Suit yourself," Adam said. At least the boy's clothes were clean. He had found an interesting little pick hidden in a seam of the shirt while he was wringing it out. He could guess its purpose. He wondered if Johnny would be willing to admit to owning it and ask for it back.

He left Johnny in the kitchen and took Peggy upstairs with him. He changed her into a clean dress and fresh white apron and combed her hair, then stood her on his dresser so she could see herself in the mirror. "Isn't Peggy pretty?"

Peggy laughed. "Nonny, come see!" she called. "Nonny!"

In seconds Johnny was bounding up the stairs, buttoning his shirt as he came. "What, baby?"

"See Peggy." She pointed at the mirror and giggled.

"Yeah, silly, that's what Peggy looks like. Didn't you know that?"

"Nonny, too." She beckoned him closer. She pointed to the Johnny that appeared in the mirror and back at her brother.

"Yep. That's me."

Adam let Peggy kiss her image goodbye, then lifted her off the dresser. While he packed Peggy's few belongings in her little case, Johnny looked around curiously. He pretended disinterest, however. Peggy followed her kitten, watching him explore.

With the case in hand, Adam directed the children back downstairs. The kitten headed toward the front room with Peggy right behind him. Johnny followed Adam into the kitchen.

"You got somethin' that belongs to me," the boy said.

"And what might that be?" Adam asked, turning to face him.

"My lock pick," he answered without a moment's hesitation.

"I don't think you need that anymore, Johnny."

"How would you know? If this family takes Peggy they ain't gonna want me. Aunt Jane ain't gonna keep feedin' me once Peggy's gone. And you can't wait till I'm outta your life."

Adam sighed. "That's not true, Johnny." He bent to gather the discarded clothes.

"The hell it ain't."

"Johnny, this family would be more likely to want you if you'd watch your language." He shook out the shirt and turned a pant leg right side out. Something heavy hit the floor at his feet.

Johnny started forward, but Adam reached it first. He turned the brand-new pocketknife slowly in his hand. Peggy's call from upstairs had evidently caused the boy to leave it in the borrowed pants.

"Now you got two things that are mine."

"Where did you get this, Johnny?" The last thing he expected was an honest answer.

"I stole it yesterday." The boy's jaw set as if he dared Adam to hit him. In the strained silence, they heard Peggy giggle in the other room.

"You'll have to return it," Adam said.

"Like hell! It's mine now."

Adam shook his head. "No. It still belongs to the store you stole it from."

Johnny grinned in triumph. "Then that pick's still mine."

Adam chuckled. "All right. The pick's still yours. I'll give it back to you, but I'll take it again if you ever use it. There's a big difference between stealing from a store and confiscating from a criminal."

"Oh, now I'm a criminal."

Adam tossed the pocketknife lightly in the air. "Seems like."

He put the clothes over the back of a chair and, taking Johnny's arm, walked through the house. "We're going for a walk," he told Peggy.

Peggy grabbed up the kitten and took Adam's other hand. Adam set a pace that was comfortable for the little girl. They were a block from the house before Johnny spoke. "What you gonna tell 'em?"

"*You're* going to tell them you stole the knife yesterday, and you're sorry. Then you're going to offer to sweep the floor and wash the windows to make up for it."

"I ain't sayin' no such thing."

"Sure you are." Adam smiled down at Peggy, who seemed oblivious to her brother's plight.

"Or what?"

"Or nothing. There's no choice here, Johnny. You're going to do what's right."

Johnny laughed. "Ain't ya gonna tell me you're gonna send me to jail?"

"I don't have to, Johnny." Adam released the boy's arm to bend and lift Peggy. She gave him a half hug around the kitten. He lengthened his steps a little just as Johnny slowed, as if he considered running. Adam stopped and waited for him. "How much do you want to stay with your sister?"

"That ain't fair," Johnny said, catching up.

"Maybe not, but it's effective."

"I don't trust you anyhow, you know. I could turn over the knife, and you could still send her away from me."

"It's not always easy to figure out who to trust." Adam found himself thinking of Jane as he said it. "Take the storekeeper. He trusted his customers to pay for what they took. How's he going to trust you to do anything you promise?"

"'Cause he figures you'll beat me if I don't?" Johnny guessed.

Adam sighed. "You're supposed to say because he knows you're honestly sorry you stole from him."

Johnny was silent for a moment. "You got a funny way a lookin' at things."

They were approaching the business district and Adam asked, "Which store, Johnny?"

"Maybe I don't want to tell you."

"Fine," he said. "We'll just start with the first store and ask."

Johnny stepped forward. "It was that one." He pointed toward Gardener's General Store.

Inside, Peggy and her kitten both squirmed to be released. They were the only customers in the store at the moment and got the full attention of both Mr. and Mrs. Gardener.

"Look, Earl," the Mrs. said. "It's the children that were here yesterday with Miss Sparks."

"Morning, Dr. Hart," said Earl.

Adam took the knife from his pocket and handed it to Johnny, nudging him forward. The boy cast him a scowl that didn't quite cover the fear in his eyes.

"Yesterday." He stopped and cleared his throat, then went on in a rush. "I stole this knife." He held it out to Mr. Gardener.

Mr. Gardener hesitated a moment before he took it. "Lila?"

His wife scurried over to a small display. "Yes, one's missing," she said.

Adam gave Johnny another nudge.

"I'm sorry I stole it, and I'll sweep up if'n you want." This last was said with a marked lack of enthusiasm.

"And…" Adam prompted.

"And wash the windows."

"What a nice boy," Lila said, joining her husband.

Adam had serious doubts about that assessment. He listened to the tap of Peggy's shoes, hoping that as long as she was moving she wasn't getting into anything.

"Maybe you'd like to work here until you can buy the knife," suggested Mr. Gardener.

"We're not sure where the boy will be living," Adam said. "He may be too far out in the country. But he can sweep up now." Adam hoped they got the hint that he thought making Johnny work for an hour or so would be a good idea.

The Gardners looked at each other. Earl made the decision. ''He could stock some shelves for us. Can you find your own way home, after?''

Adam couldn't help laughing. ''I think that's the least of our worries.'' He turned to Johnny and patted him down. ''When you get back, your pockets better be just as empty as they are now.''

Johnny made a face, then turned to the couple. ''Tell me what to do. The sooner I get started the sooner I'm done.''

Adam found Peggy following the kitten around the shelves. He checked her apron pocket but needn't have worried. There wasn't room for any pilfered items because it contained half a biscuit.

Peggy slung the kitten over one arm and let Adam lift her. When they walked out the door, she pointed over his shoulder. ''Nonny.''

''Johnny's going to work here for a little while.''

''Peggy, too.''

''No,'' Adam said, heading for home. ''Peggy needs to come home with me. There are some people coming who'll want to meet you.''

''Nonny gone?''

''No, he'll be along.''

He answered the same question a dozen more times. By the time he reached the house, the question had become a whisper. Peggy headed straight for the desk and hid.

* * *

Jane couldn't keep her mind off Adam and the children. She wanted to run next door and hug them one more time. She wanted to be there when the prospective parents came for them, but she understood why she couldn't.

When the dishes were clean and put away, she went out to her garden. After digging sweet potatoes for dinner, she returned to her kitchen, feeling no interest in any pruning or weeding.

Now, she decided, was the time to read her mother's letters. They had been working on her curiosity since she had found them. She considered the parlor, as it was sunny this time of day, but didn't want to be disturbed. She flung open the curtains in her bedroom and settled into a chair by the window, the packet on her lap.

Peggy wouldn't venture out from under the desk, although the kitten did. Adam thought she would eventually follow the kitten, but instead her loud whisper would call the kitten back to their hiding place. Adam wished Peggy was really playing the game the kitten took it for. How was he to explain this behavior to prospective parents?

Fortunately, Johnny returned about midday and coaxed her out. "You don't have to hide anymore. I told ya," he said.

"Nonny gone," she whimpered, clinging to him.

"I weren't gone. I was workin'. Wanna see what I got?"

Peggy nodded vigorously.

Johnny fished around in his pocket and pulled out a penny. He smiled as he showed it to his sister, then turned a defiant glare on Adam. "I didn't steal it, neither. If'n I was to steal, I'd know enough to take more'n a penny."

"That's probably the most convincing evidence you could give me," Adam said. "Are you hungry?"

He led the way to the kitchen, where he laid out a light lunch of cheese and crackers. Peggy put the kitten down and climbed into a chair. "Nonny fat," she announced.

"Not this Nonny," Johnny said.

"Nonny Kitty," said Peggy, pointing.

"Is Peggy fat, too?" Johnny asked, tickling her ribs. "If you're gettin' fat it's Aunt Jane's doin', not Dr. Hart's."

Peggy giggled. "Go see Ann Jane."

"Maybe later," Adam said, hoping to divert the girl's attention. "Have a cracker."

"Go see Ann Jane," she repeated, taking the cracker and biting into it.

Johnny smirked at him, and he knew there would be no help there. "We can't, honey. Aunt Jane's busy."

"Ann Jane gone?" she asked, looking concerned.

"Aunt Jane's working, like Johnny was."

This seemed to satisfy her, and she settled into the chair and ate. When she was full, she dropped the crumbling biscuit from her pocket onto the floor for Nonny and replaced it with crackers and cheese. Johnny was more secretive, but Adam noticed he put a little away in his pockets as well. It made Adam wonder if the boy was waiting for a chance to run away.

Before they had finished cleaning up from their lunch, George came in the front door, calling, "Adam?"

Adam quickly brushed the worst of the crumbs off Peggy's face and dress and brought the two children out to meet him.

"Adam," George announced, "this is Mr. and Mrs. Dobbs. Folks, this is Dr. Hart and little Peggy and Johnny."

Adam shot Johnny a warning look and shook hands with the couple. They were middle-aged and seemed very pleasant.

"We didn't know about the boy," the wife said. "I was just wanting a girl."

"We didn't know about Johnny, either," Adam said. "He traveled a long way to find his sister. I believe they ought to stay together."

"He doesn't look very strong," the husband commented. "Is he willing to work?"

Adam wondered how Johnny felt hearing himself discussed. The boy was frowning at his sister.

"I think he'd do anything for his sister," Adam said. "And that would include working hard so he could stay near her."

"I don't know," the wife said. "I only wanted a girl."

"We could keep him as labor," her husband suggested. "He could sleep in the barn."

Adam didn't like that idea at all, but before he could speak, Johnny sprang to his feet.

"Ma'am," he said, still looking at his sister. "If you just want a girl you can take her. You don't need to find no place for me." He finally looked at the couple. "But you better love her and be good to her."

"Well, it's settled then," the woman said, smiling. She knelt down. "Do you want to come home with me, little girl?"

In Adam's mind, this was far from settled. He didn't want to send Peggy home with people who would even talk of treating Johnny as merely labor. He was ready to object when Peggy did it for him.

"No," she said.

"You go with 'em, Peggy," Johnny said. His eyes were dry but there were tears in his voice. "They'll be your mama and papa." He gave her a nudge toward the woman.

Peggy ran to Adam instead and grabbed his leg. She pointed a little finger at the woman and yelled, "You go!"

The woman drew back, offended. "I understood she was a quiet, sweet child."

Adam put his hand on her shoulder. "She is. You've just frightened her. But maybe it's for the best. I don't want her to go without Johnny, and I don't want Johnny sleeping in a barn.''

George made the apologies and saw the couple out the door. When he turned back, he was smiling. "You ready to give up, son?''

Adam lifted Peggy into his arms. "It's not a matter of giving up," he muttered. "It's—''

Peggy's sticky hands turned his face toward her, cutting him off. "Go see Ann Jane?''

Adam ignored George's laugh. "Johnny, take Peggy outside, please, but try not to let her bother Aunt Jane.''

Johnny had been watching him curiously. "How do I do that?'' he asked, taking his sister's hand when Adam set her down.

"I don't know. Keep her outside.''

Johnny scowled at him over his shoulder. "You're gonna talk about me, ain't ya?''

The letters were scattered on the floor all around Jane's chair. She had read every one through at least twice. Her first surprise had been discovering that they were from her father, even the letters with the obviously feminine handwriting on the envelope. Her father's fear that Grams would destroy any letters from him had forced him to ask a neighbor for assistance.

Jane's second surprise had been to learn that her father had loved her mother and, according to the references to her responses, she had loved him in return. He had not abandoned his family; Grams had torn it apart.

Grams, in her anger at her own abandonment, had discouraged Hanna's love for William. When that had not been successful, she had feigned illness to bring her daughter home. Once back under her mother's influence, Hanna had never been able to break away again. Time after time, William had asked when Hanna would come back to him. He had begged to be allowed to come get her, to at least visit her and their little girl.

Jane wondered if Grams had written to him when Hanna died. The last letter was dated months before that, but he might have written again, a letter that Grams opened to discover from whom it had come. If that was the case, Grams would have learned that Hanna had not been corresponding with a female friend, after all. Had Grams searched for the other letters among Hanna's things? Perhaps not or she wouldn't have dismissed the jewelry box.

It was hard to reconcile the woman referred to in the letters with the grandmother Jane had known all her life. Grams had loved her and cared for her, but she had also lied to her. She had taught her to mistrust men, claiming that her father had been just like her grandfather. Jane had to wonder, now, if her grandfather had been as bad as Grams had claimed.

But none of that mattered as much as the present. Her grandmother's teachings had led her to mistrust Adam. How miserably she had treated him! He had told her he loved her and she had thrown the words right back in his face.

She had no idea how to make amends. She had fought him over the children until he thought they were all she cared about. They were probably even now heading for their new home. Adam must think she could never forgive him.

She hadn't allowed herself to try to understand why he had prevented her from taking Peggy. She had assumed that he couldn't be trusted to have her interests in mind. She had believed her grandmother.

She bent and gathered the letters into a neat stack and retied the ribbon around them. She wouldn't let her grandmother's bitterness ruin her life the way it had her mother's. But exactly where she should start was a question she didn't know how to answer.

She left her bedroom, glancing at the clock in the parlor as she went by. It was already past noon. She should fix herself a lunch and start the pies for dinner.

As she entered the kitchen she heard a muffled argument outside her door. A familiar voice rose to a demand. "See Ann Jane!"

She swung open the door to find Johnny urging Peggy away from her back steps. Both children fell silent when they saw her.

Peggy held up her kitten. "Nonny fat," she announced, grinning.

"Dr. Hart said not to bother Aunt Jane," Johnny

reminded his sister. "Seems like we're always botherin' somebody."

"Oh, pooh," Jane said. "When were you ever a bother?"

Johnny's answering grin didn't have quite the defiant edge she had seen before. "I don't think I wanna say."

Jane laughed, taking the kitten, which was showing signs of resenting being held in the air. "Do you want to come inside?"

Johnny glanced toward the house next door. "We better not."

It occurred to Jane that their prospective parents might even now be conferring with Adam. She sat on the step and tried for a cheerful voice when she asked, "Has the family come to meet you yet?"

"Come and gone," Johnny said, digging a toe into the dirt.

"Gone?" She hadn't been entirely successful at keeping the elation out of her voice.

Johnny grinned suddenly. "Peggy wouldn't have 'em. Told 'em to go away."

"Oh, dear. Were they so awful?" She tried for a sympathetic tone, but she wanted to laugh out loud.

"Pretty awful. They was real old, and she didn't want no boy. He said they'd keep me in the barn."

Jane hugged Peggy. She would have hugged Johnny, too, but he kept out of reach. "I'm glad you told them to go away," she said. "There'll be better chances for a family, someone who wants you both.''

Johnny gave a derisive laugh. ''When Ma's last boyfriend hit Peggy I decided I didn't want no family.''

Jane reached a hand toward him but he side-stepped, studying his toes. ''It was gonna be just her and me, but I can't take care of her. I thought I could, but I can't.''

''Don't even think about running away,'' she said softly. His head jerked up, and his startled expression told her she had read his mind. ''You'd break Peggy's heart. And mine.''

Peggy's head turned to the side, and she squirmed out of Jane's embrace. Adam was striding across the yards, and the little girl ran to meet him. ''See Ann Jane,'' she directed.

Adam swept her up in his arms, and she squealed with delight. ''Yes, I see you found Aunt Jane.''

Jane stood as he walked toward her. She felt like she was seeing him for the first time, seeing him for who he was, not what she had been taught to see. What she saw made her heart skip. He was handsome, as she had noticed before, but the kindness that she had never let herself believe seemed so obvious to her now.

He joined them by the back door, hugging Peggy again before he set her on her feet to follow her wandering kitten. ''Did they tell you about Mr. and Mrs. Dobbs?''

"A little," Jane said. She noticed Johnny shied away, as if he expected to be blamed for something. She wondered if he had been less than truthful about their reason for rejecting Peggy.

Adam sighed. "They weren't what we hoped for."

He hesitated a moment. "I hate to ask this, but could the children stay here this afternoon? I've got a call and it sounds like another case of the flu. I had two yesterday and heard of a few more. It's nothing too serious, but I don't want them exposed."

"Of course," Jane said. "Is there anything I can do?"

Adam laughed. "Are you going to make enough chicken soup for the whole town?"

She tried not to smile. "I just might."

"Well, don't. Not yet, because the whole town isn't sick. I need to run. I'll be back as soon as I can." He turned to Johnny. "Help watch your sister, all right?"

Johnny wasn't quite fast enough to avoid the squeeze on his shoulder. It didn't seem to be what he was expecting.

As Adam started back across the yard, Peggy ran after him. "Docka Hart!"

Adam stopped and crouched before her. He gave her a hug and whispered something in her ear. She nodded. He turned her around and gave her a light pat on the back. She skipped off after her kitten. As he stood, he waved to Jane and Johnny.

Jane found herself staring after him long after he had gone back inside. It was Johnny who brought her back to her senses. "You wantin' a hug goodbye, too?"

Jane felt her cheeks flame. "Johnny!"

He laughed. "You look at Dr. Hart like Nonny looks at a bowl a cream."

Chapter Fourteen

It was George who mentioned the flu at dinner. He had heard of several cases from people coming into the bank. There was even a rumor, he said, that it was really cholera. "They've canceled church services this morning," he added.

Adam shook his head. "No, it's just influenza. Rumors could cause a panic worse than the disease itself."

"I've heard there have been three deaths," George added before suggesting that the platter of beef be passed around again.

Adam wondered if this was another rumor or if there were deaths he didn't know about. He was still new here, and not everyone trusted doctors. "There's been one death. The elder Mr. Bartlett."

He glanced around the table. The Cartland sisters and young Ferris Wood were watching him with alarm. Bickford didn't look quite as bored as usual.

Jane was trying to distract the children from the conversation and listen to it at the same time.

"I didn't hear names," George admitted. "Bartlett was an old man. He had to die of something."

"Well, yes," Adam conceded. "Influenza is always hardest on the elderly, very young and those already weakened by some other cause."

George poured gravy on another scoop of potatoes. "I've already heard speculation that the orphans brought the disease, and it spread at that gathering."

He gave a quick glance toward Peggy, and Adam realized folks would remember her falling ill during the presentation. It didn't help that she was in his care. Some might hesitate to seek his advice because of Peggy.

Certain someone would come to his home carrying the illness, Adam asked Jane to keep the children all the time. He discovered rather quickly that he missed them. He was often out on a call at mealtime, but stopped in to see them once or twice a day if at all possible. He told Jane that he needed to make sure Johnny was staying out of trouble. He admitted to himself that he was missing Jane as well.

He had worried that the children would wear Jane out, but she seemed to be holding up better than he was. She never complained about them. In fact, from her reports one would think they were perfect angels. Johnny occasionally admitted to some minor mischief, as if Jane were ruining his reputation.

Every day, Adam noticed additions to Johnny's wardrobe or Peggy's basket of toys, starting with a set of painted blocks. By midweek Johnny was wearing shoes and carrying around a reading primer. Adam hadn't thought to wonder if Johnny could read, but Jane evidently had.

Called away at all hours of the day and night, Adam left a notice on his door as to whose house he was visiting. Often he was tracked down and taken directly from one home to another. He gave up horseback riding and rented a buggy so he could sleep on the way back to town.

Jane was so grateful for the children. She worried about Adam anyway, of course, but not with the overwhelming anxiety she might have. Johnny and Peggy simply kept her too busy. Peggy was a very happy, energetic child. It was a bit of a challenge to keep her occupied.

Johnny had his moments of restlessness, as well. Jane tried to give him a few responsibilities to make him feel needed, but he was quick to detect any that were unnecessary. Shopping for her seemed to be his greatest joy. The first time she handed him a few coins and asked him to run to the store for something, he hadn't been able to hide his surprise. Now she tried to forget at least one important item when she shopped.

Each time she set the table, she wondered if Adam would be there to eat with them. When he wasn't, she kept food warm on the stove, in case he came later. If he hadn't arrived by the children's bedtime, she and the children took dinner to his kitchen, lit a fire in his stove and left the food there.

When he did join them, he told of homes smelling of onions, which were supposed to cleanse the atmosphere, of children sleeping in the same bed as their sick siblings, and of mothers, exhausted from caring for ill children, taking to their beds with even worse cases of the disease.

Jane wished for it to be over. When she took the children with her to shop, she noticed worried glances leveled at Peggy. It wouldn't be long until the children noticed them, too. Other children were no longer allowed to play in her backyard. Though she knew this was wise, that children together were likely to pass the flu around, she also knew it was primarily because of Peggy that the children weren't allowed to come.

One morning, a week into the epidemic, Ferris didn't come down for breakfast. No one seemed particularly alarmed. "It's Sunday." George said. "He doesn't have to work today."

Much as a young man his age might like to sleep, Jane knew he also liked to eat. She couldn't recall a single meal he had missed since he had arrived. When the others were finished, she left Johnny in charge of Peggy and went up to Ferris's room.

Her light tap on the door got no response. She knocked louder and heard a groan. Perhaps Ferris had been out celebrating the previous night and was paying the price this morning. But that didn't sound like Ferris.

Jane opened the door a crack. "We missed you at breakfast," she said gently, mindful that he might have a headache.

He groaned again. "I'd rather die than eat," he said plaintively. "Did the doctor come to breakfast?"

"No, I'm sorry. He'll be around sometime today, I'm sure. You've caught the flu, haven't you?"

Ferris nodded weakly.

Jane stepped up to the bed and placed a hand on the young man's forehead, gauging his temperature. "I'll bring you some water and a cool cloth."

He nodded again.

Poor Ferris was not much more than a boy and far away from his family. She left him and returned to her kitchen.

"Ferris is sick," she told the children. "Play as quietly as you can and don't go upstairs."

"Upstairs?" Johnny was incredulous. "With them Cartland women livin' up there, you couldn't make me go up them stairs. Peggy neither."

Peggy shook her head. "Neither."

"Good," Jane said. "It wouldn't be fun to be sick like Ferris."

"It wouldn't be fun to be chased away by them Cartland women, neither."

"Neither!" Peggy said.

Jane checked on Ferris several times as the day

passed. By midafternoon, Peggy started to ask after Adam every few minutes, needing to be reassured that "Docka Hart" wasn't gone forever.

Jane set a place for Adam at the table, but none for Ferris. The Cartlands noticed immediately. "He's down with the flu," Jane told them.

"The flu! My dear woman," Nedra said, "we should have been told."

"I don't know what you could have done," Jane said, knowing there was little chance she would volunteer to sit with the boy.

"Done?" chimed in Naomi. "We would have left."

"Left?" Jane found herself holding her breath. The others, including George, were standing beside their chairs waiting for the women to be seated.

"We most assuredly can't stay here," Nedra agreed.

"We must pack up at once."

They eyed the table a moment, then reached a decision simultaneously, taking their places. They weren't in so big a hurry to leave as to pass up dinner.

Jane took her seat also, casting a questioning glance at George. He knew how important it was that they stay.

"I don't think you need to do anything hasty," he said. "Besides, where would you go?"

"We may just go to Ames," Naomi said. "There's a hotel there. We might take our business there, as well. The prospects here haven't been what we were hoping for, anyway.''

Nedra immediately agreed. "We can pack up after dinner and still catch the evening train.''

It must have been worry that brought to Jane's lips exactly what she was thinking. "Isn't it nice you never got around to ordering any merchandise for your shop? So much easier to move this way.''

The women looked at her, aghast. George chuckled and tried to cover it with a cough. "Five miles isn't far enough to escape the flu, ladies. You might end up next door to another case.''

"*Might* is the key word,'' Naomi said. "Here it's definite. Besides, at the hotel we won't be eating with the carrier.'' She leveled her glare at Peggy, who stared back, horrified. Johnny bent and whispered in his sister's ear. They both giggled, and Peggy went back to her dinner. Naomi's eyes narrowed, and she gave an audible sniff.

Jane ate the rest of the meal in silence. There were no words she could think of to make the Cartlands change their minds, especially after her own remark. By the time they had finished dessert, the ladies had talked themselves into believing they were about to embark on an adventure as grand as their original move to Clyde.

Two empty rooms. Jane's budget had not allowed for this. It would be difficult, but perhaps not impossible, to make the next payment. She could rely on her own garden a little more and save at the grocer's. But she would have to fill those two rooms as soon as possible.

George lingered a moment after the boarders had gone. "There's no need to worry, Jane," he said.

She assumed he was speaking of their vulnerability to the flu. No, she and the children were healthy. They would be fine.

Jane sent the children out to play in the yard and took some broth up to Ferris. She had a feeling the boy would have liked her to stay with him, and she did for as long as she felt she could. She considered moving him downstairs, to Grams's old sickroom, but didn't want him that close to the children. After feeding him as much broth as he would take, and sponging off his fevered face, she placed the cool cloth across his forehead and left, promising to return soon.

She was half finished with the dishes when she heard the Cartlands on the stairs. She dried her hands and went to see them off, determined to collect half a month's rent. They had the money ready, figured to the day.

"We'll send someone over for the trunks," Nedra said.

That was as much of a farewell as they were going to give Jane. She tried to be gracious and wished them luck.

They were no sooner out the door than Lawrence Bickford descended the stairs, his suitcase in hand.

"You're leaving also?" she asked in surprise.

"Naomi convinced me."

Of course. Jane should have thought of that.

Bickford at least had included a small tip in his payment. "The school board has postponed the opening of classes because of the epidemic. I'll return before the term begins," he said.

She wouldn't be here by then, she thought. The loss of his rent left too much of a hole in her finances. The bank would own the building in approximately two weeks. Her revenge, she thought, could be applying for his job, but that wasn't really what she wanted.

Disconsolate, she returned to the kitchen. What else could she have done? She couldn't have turned poor Ferris out. The boy had no one to count on except for her and George.

The children came in as it started to get dark. They had been waiting for Adam, she learned, missing him as much as she was.

"Docka Hart gone," Peggy said sadly.

Johnny rolled his eyes. "You can't explain nothin' to her."

"He'll come back," Jane said, lifting the child. But she was worried, too. What if he had fallen ill somewhere, perhaps along a lonely road? Peggy must have felt some of her distress because she put her head on Jane's shoulder and started to cry.

"Brother!" Johnny grabbed his book and sat down at the kitchen table. "She used to be fine when it was just us. Now she's got to have everybody she knows right beside her all the time.''

"She's only little,'' Jane said, rocking the sobbing child, wanting to cry as well. Her home, her business were gone. Her last boarder was upstairs sick and lonely. Adam had been gone all day. She was worried about him, she wanted to tell him all her troubles and she just plain wanted to see him again.

"Docka Hart gone!'' Peggy wailed.

"Shut up, you stupid baby!''

"Johnny,'' Jane admonished gently. The strain was wearing on him, too. "Babies only cry louder if you tell them to shut up.''

Peggy was willingly proving her point.

"Will she shut up if I tell her to cry louder? She's hurtin' my ears.''

"What's all this?''

Adam. Jane nearly wilted in relief. She hadn't heard the door open and close for all the noise. "Look who's here,'' she said, wiping her hand across Peggy's damp face.

Peggy let out three more shuddering sobs as she reached for Adam. He took her from Jane, murmuring softly, "What's the great tragedy?''

"Docka Hart gone,'' she whimpered.

"Oh, that. When Johnny goes missing at least you're quiet.''

Peggy clung to him, her face at the crook of his neck. Jane wanted to lean on the other shoulder and cry, too. She smiled at him, instead. It was good to see him, but he looked even worse than she felt. She couldn't burden him with her troubles after the day he must have had.

"Sit down. I'll get you some dinner."

He sat across from Johnny with Peggy nestled in his lap. Jane listened to them talk about the reading primer while she warmed up the chicken, potatoes and gravy she had saved.

It was wonderful to have Adam in her kitchen. It felt as if he had set everything to rights again. She knew he hadn't, of course. She had still lost her boarders, and unless a miracle happened, she would lose the house soon, as well.

But the children had both been upset a moment ago. She had felt a wave of desperation herself. Now Johnny was proudly pointing out which letters he had learned and the few words he could recognize, and Peggy was giggling and playing Adam's echo. For the moment it felt like they were a family. Almost home. Like the name of her boardinghouse, it wasn't quite the real thing.

She set Adam's dinner in front of him. He thanked her as he helped Peggy slide off his lap. "Get Aunt Jane a chair," he said to Johnny.

"Have mine," Johnny said, very politely. He sat down on the floor near his sister's basket of toys and stuck his nose in his book.

"How was your day?" Adam asked.

It was so much in keeping with Jane's fantasy that

she almost laughed. "Not good, but I'll wager yours was worse. You look terrible."

"Thanks," he said, grinning. "Does exhaustion make me look older?"

Now she did laugh. "That and the fact that you forgot to shave."

"I didn't exactly forget. I delivered a baby early this morning." He was still grinning that little-boy grin she hadn't seen in a long time. "That was good."

"Was it?" she asked, wanting to encourage the light in his eyes that warmed her all the way to her toes.

"Yeah. It would have been better if they'd waited about four hours to get me, but it was good." The smile faded and he looked down at his plate. "Everything went downhill after that."

"More flu victims?"

He nodded. She didn't press for details. "I hate to tell you this, but you've got one more patient to look in on tonight."

He raised his head, his expression questioning.

"Ferris came down with it sometime last night."

Adam glanced at the children. Jane could guess what he was thinking. "I'm keeping them away from him."

He nodded. His eyes stayed on her for a long moment. "You can't know how important it is for me to have you to come back to."

Jane blinked. Johnny gave a little chortle, but

when they turned to look his face was hidden in the book. Adam returned his attention to his food, rather self-consciously, she thought. She had to school her features to keep from smiling at him. Maybe he forgave her for being so suspicious of his motives.

After he had eaten and looked in on Ferris, he helped her get the children ready for bed. "I'd take them home with me," he said, "but who knows when I'll get called away again. I hate to leave them alone."

"You think I'll run away, don't ya?" Johnny remarked.

Adam handed Johnny a toothbrush he'd dipped in baking soda. "It crossed my mind."

"I think I waited too long. I'll never get her away from you two now."

"I'm glad to know you won't leave without her. I don't want to spend another morning with her under my desk. Now brush your teeth."

Johnny stuck the toothbrush in his mouth and pulled it back out. "What *are* you gonna do with us?"

Jane slid the little nightgown over Peggy's head and looked up at Adam. She was as curious as Johnny about the answer to that question. Of course, her situation had changed. She no longer had a home to offer them or the means to support them.

Adam's eyes met Jane's for a moment. "As soon as we figure it out, we'll let you know," he said to

Johnny. "In the meantime, we'll be sure you're safe and well fed. You don't need to worry."

"Oh, that sure as hell relieves my mind," Johnny said around the toothbrush.

"It's the best I can do, Johnny."

Jane wondered just what kind of hoops she had to jump through to get Adam to let her have the children. He didn't know about the defection of the boarders. He simply didn't think she was able to care for them. She smiled at the sleepy Peggy, pretending not to be hurt by Adam's words.

She kept the same smile on her face as the children were tucked into the little bed. She managed to say good-night to Adam and see him out the door without a single tear escaping. But she made it only halfway to her own bedroom before they started to fall.

Jane took a leaf out of her table before she set it for breakfast. It didn't look quite as empty that way. She could have taken out another. Adam had been called away again.

George reported what Adam hadn't told her the evening before—that there had been two more deaths from influenza. Everybody who came into his bank, it seemed, had a story to tell about one epidemic or another that they had survived, witnessed or imagined. These stories were being repeated, confused and combined.

"I'm glad to know Adam was still kickin' as of

last night," George said. "Don't see how he's going to keep from coming down with this before it's over."

Jane had been thinking the same thing. In his current state of exhaustion, he was probably highly susceptible.

"How's our patient upstairs?" George asked.

"He seems to be doing all right," Jane said, "but he's lonely. I can't stay with him all the time. I can't ask anyone else to, either."

"I'll see if I can't cheer him up a little," George said.

George visited with Ferris for several minutes after breakfast while Johnny helped Jane with the dishes. "How come you ain't worried about gettin' sick?" Johnny asked.

"To be honest, I am, just a little. On the other hand, I can't ignore someone like Ferris, who has no one else to take care of him."

"Kinda like why you take care of me."

Jane turned from the pan of dishes and looked at the boy. He wouldn't meet her eyes. "Is that what you think—that I see you as a duty?"

The boy shuffled his feet. "I know you was wantin' a little girl, but now I come along and you ain't so sure you want us both."

"Where on earth did you get that idea?" Jane dried her hands on her apron and squatted down in front of the boy.

"You mean you don't want Peggy, neither?"

Jane shook her head. "Couldn't you tell how delighted I was that that family didn't take you? And I thought you were such a clever boy." He wasn't to be teased out of his concern. She continued, "We don't always get what we want, but I'll do everything I can to keep you both."

This satisfied Johnny for the moment, but not Jane. Just what could she do to keep the children? Find a job and a house she could afford. She had about two weeks to do it. Maybe a little longer; George had always been more than reasonable.

She would start right away by buying a newspaper to see who was hiring and who had rooms to rent. Selling part of her furniture would raise a little money. It hurt to think of leaving this house behind, but not as much as losing the children. She had to be practical.

"Let's go shopping," she said, when the dishes were done.

Peggy had been playing with the blocks in the corner. Other than a glance occasionally to see that she was still there, Jane hadn't paid much attention to her. Now she realized that Peggy wasn't playing. She merely sat, holding one block on her lap, ignoring the kitten as it chewed on her dress.

"Peggy?" Jane knelt down beside her.

Peggy looked up, her eyes overbright and bleary. Jane was almost afraid to touch her. She had a sudden flash of Grams, sick and dying. There was the same fever in her eyes.

Chapter Fifteen

Jane sent Johnny over to Adam's to see if he was home. She was almost certain he wasn't, or he would have come to breakfast. *Maybe he's sleeping late. Maybe he's only just returned.*

She gathered the little girl into her arms and carried her to the bed. Peggy made her think of a rag doll as she removed her shoes and dress.

Jane tried to keep her voice cheerful as she talked to the child. "When did you start to feel bad, sweetheart?"

"Bad Peggy," she moaned.

"No," Jane soothed. "Peggy's my little sweetheart."

She pulled a cool sheet over Peggy and got the basin and a clean cloth. She sat beside her, sponging the cool cloth over Peggy's hot face. This was horribly familiar. She told herself not to think about Grams. This wasn't the same, but she couldn't control her imagination.

Johnny came back and stood in the doorway. "He ain't there."

She looked up to thank him and realized there was something more he wanted to say. "What is it, Johnny?"

"There's a note on his door, only I can't read it. I expect it says where he's gone."

"I'm sure that's right," she said.

Jane thought she heard him sniff once. "Only I can't read so I can't find him."

Jane laid the cloth across Peggy's forehead and rose. She pulled Johnny into her arms and held him. She could feel him fighting back sobs. "Is she gonna die?"

"Of course not. Dr. Hart says healthy people recover quite easily."

"But Peggy's a baby."

She pulled Johnny away to look him in the eye. "She's not really a baby. And she's strong. I don't want you to worry."

"You're worried," he accused.

There was no lying to this child. "I shouldn't be," she told him, smiling. "You and I can't help it because we love her."

Johnny took a deep breath. "I could take the note to that George fella. He knows everybody. I could find Dr. Hart."

"Out on the open prairie?"

The boy shuddered. "I could try."

"I'm sure you would succeed. But I think I need

you here more than we really need Dr. Hart.'' Jane
prayed that was true. Adam had told her the evening
before that she had been doing all there was to do
for Ferris. She would do the same for Peggy.

"I need to take some soup up to Ferris," she continued. "I want you to stay here in the kitchen and
call for me if Peggy needs anything. Don't get too
close to her, or you might get sick, too."

"Too close to her? I slept with her last night."

"Well, last night she wasn't sick. I'll only be a
few minutes."

Ferris was feeling sorry for himself. He was cold,
then he was hot. His head hurt and his throat hurt,
in fact his whole body hurt. He couldn't breathe if
he lay down, but he felt too weak to sit up. Jane got
two extra pillows for him out of the now-vacant
rooms. She fed him the soup, left him a fresh glass
of water and found him the book he wanted to read.
She left feeling relatively sure that there were no
signs of anything worse than the flu.

Downstairs she found Johnny sitting on the bed,
his sister on his lap. He rocked her back and forth.
The look he threw Jane dared her to send him away.
There wasn't any use now, anyway, she decided.
Besides, having him near seemed to make Peggy
feel better.

Jane divided her time between Peggy and Ferris.
By midafternoon she drew Johnny away from his
sister long enough to take a message to George, telling him she wouldn't be serving dinner that night.

He stopped by shortly afterward with a magazine for Ferris, which he kept rolled up until he took it upstairs. Jane suspected it might be less than wholesome reading, and probably exactly what Ferris needed to lift his spirits.

For Peggy he brought a Jacob's ladder toy, the six wooden pieces held together with bright ribbons. Johnny had never seen anything like it and tried to figure out how it worked. Peggy seemed content to watch her brother make the blocks clatter their way to the bottom.

Once George had left there was little to do but worry. The flu could, and had in some cases, turned into pneumonia. Jane was well aware of the danger of that disease. She did her best to hide her worry from Johnny, and Johnny in turn tried to be brave for Peggy's sake.

At the usual dinner hour, she coaxed Johnny to the kitchen table. She had boiled another chicken for broth for the flu victims and had fixed the meat with noodles. There was plenty, of course, in case Adam arrived. She had even set a place at the table for him.

Johnny eyed the empty chair as he took his seat. Jane sat across from him. They ate in silence, listening to Peggy snore and occasionally cough. In the quiet, they heard the door open.

Jane was out of her seat and in Adam's arms before she even stopped to think. The strength of those arms and the masculine, prairie-wind scent of him brought her to her senses. She tried to pull away, embarrassed, but he didn't let her go immediately.

"I see Peggy's teaching you how to say hello." He drew away enough to look into Jane's eyes. He was, of course, grinning.

Jane chewed on her lip. If she laughed she'd start to cry. "Peggy's sick," she managed to say.

He let her go, or rather almost did. He kept her hand in his and turned to the little bedroom. "When?" he asked.

"After breakfast. She's hot and fussy. She coughs and her voice sounds funny."

Adam touched his palm gently to her forehead and brushed a lock of fine hair away from her face. "Let's let her sleep." He turned back into the kitchen. "I practically ran that poor horse to death to get back here for dinner."

His arm went around Jane's shoulder, whether for comfort or to draw her away from Peggy, Jane wasn't sure. It felt very nice. No, it was better than that. With him here, she could almost believe everything would be all right.

Until recently she had believed she must keep her deepest worries hidden from Adam, that he would take advantage of her if he knew what made her vulnerable. Now she wanted nothing more than to pour out her heart to him. His calm strength made him seem capable of carrying the whole world on his shoulders.

She had opened up to him once before. He had

learned about her childhood and told her about
Doreena. And where had it led? She felt her cheeks
grow warm and covered it by quickly sliding into
her seat and raising her coffee cup. That was not
what she should be thinking about with Johnny at
the table and Peggy lying sick in the next room.

After dinner the few dishes were quickly washed
and put away. Adam checked in on Ferris, while
Jane talked Johnny into sleeping in the parlor. He
brushed off any concern that he might become ill
but gave in when Jane suggested that Peggy would
sleep better by herself. When she apologized for the
discomfort of the narrow couch, he assured her he
had slept on worse.

Johnny took twice as long as usual to get ready
for bed. Jane assumed he wanted to stay close to his
sister, but when Adam came down he asked to speak
to him alone, man to man.

Jane couldn't hide her curiosity as they went off
to the parlor together. She moved a chair into
Peggy's bedroom, prepared to sit beside the little
girl all night.

Adam was grinning when he walked back through
the dining room. He had kept a straight face during
the boy's conversation, of course, agreeing quite
happily to everything he asked. Adam wasn't sure
how to break the news to Jane, however.

He found her with Peggy, no surprise there. "You
should let her sleep," he said softly.

"What if she gets worse in the night?"

He didn't bother arguing, but moved another chair to the far side of the bed. "Johnny asked me to stay."

She looked up and smiled. There was no lamp in the room, but one burned on the table in the kitchen. Though a little twilight came through the window, he saw her mostly in soft shadows.

"I feel better just knowing you're here, Adam," she said.

"I've heard that a time or two the last few days." He leaned forward to press his palm against Peggy's forehead. She shifted a little in the bed and sighed. "There's not much I can do but offer reassurance."

The kitten scampered into the bedroom, undaunted by the darkness. After checking out the occupants he was off again.

"You should get some sleep," Adam suggested. "I'll stay with Peggy."

"No, I wouldn't sleep, anyway."

He was glad she wanted to stay. It was pleasant having her nearby, and so rare the last few days. He'd offer again in an hour, he decided.

"It's my fault," she said after a moment. "If Peggy dies it's my fault."

He didn't like her even thinking that Peggy was in that much danger, but he decided to address that later. "How do you figure that?" he asked.

"When Ferris got sick, I shouldn't have kept the children here. It was just so nice having a family that I didn't want to part with them. She's sick because I was selfish.''

"They wouldn't have been any safer running around with me.''

"We should have found someplace else for them to stay.''

We. He was glad she wasn't taking all the blame. "That wouldn't have been easy, Jane. Almost every family has someone down with this stuff. And may I remind you, most of them are recovering.''

"I know. I believe you. But it's easy to be frightened. Especially when you're not here.''

He smiled a very self-satisfied smile he hoped she couldn't see in the dark. "Well, I'm here. So stop worrying.''

She fell silent, making no promises, he noticed.

"When I was Peggy's age,'' he said sometime later, "I would have jumped at the chance these children have, to come out west and find a family. By the time I was Johnny's age, I had convinced myself I was better off without one. I think that's how Johnny felt when he first came here.''

It didn't occur to him until he said it that he still wanted the family he had dreamed of as a little child. And that family was right here in this house.

"I think Johnny's afraid to hope for love for fear of being disappointed,'' she said.

"I suspect he's coming around.''

He had piqued her curiosity, which was his intent. "What did you two talk about?'' she asked.

"Oh, we struck a couple of bargains."

She scowled at him. He wasn't sure how he knew in the low light, but he did. She turned after a moment, wet the cloth and smoothed it back over Peggy's forehead, evidently deciding not to ask.

He was dying to tell her what Johnny wanted. It would be smarter to try his own proposal first, though. Proposal. Over a sick child in the dark. To a woman who had already said she didn't believe he loved her. And Jane thought *she* was scared.

Before he had decided on the proper approach, Jane said, "You can have the house."

The change of subject was so baffling it took him a moment to even ask her to repeat it.

"You can have the house. My boarders left yesterday. I won't be able to make the next payment."

"You think I want your house?" He was so incredulous he forgot to keep his voice down.

Peggy tried to sit up. "Docka Hart?"

"Right here, honey." He lifted her onto his lap. She was slightly warmer than she should be, but nothing like some of the cases he'd seen.

"Peggy's Docka Hart," the little girl said.

"That's right, honey." He was surprised to find a lump in his throat. "Maybe you're right," he said to Jane. "Maybe I do want this house. But I can't imagine it without you in it. Or my life without you, either."

"You, either," Peggy mimicked. She yawned,

then coughed, whimpering at the soreness in her throat.

Jane passed him the glass of water, and he got her to swallow a few sips before passing it back.

"What I'm getting at," he said, very softly, "is I'm in love with you. I think I fell in love with you even before Doreena was wise enough to break our engagement."

Jane's voice was even softer than his had been. It was almost a hiss. "If that's true, if you loved me, why would you keep me from getting Peggy?"

"I was afraid you'd work yourself into exhaustion."

She was quiet for a moment, then asked, "Are you still?"

"Oh, certainly," he said without hesitation. "But I've seen a good many mothers the last few days. It seems to go with the territory."

"So what are you saying?"

Adam stood and eased Peggy back onto the bed. "We're not helping Peggy, we're just keeping her awake. Let's move into the kitchen."

Jane was reluctant to follow him. She fussed with Peggy's covers until Adam took her arm and drew her out of the room. He suspected she was less worried about Peggy at the moment than what he had to say. He directed her to a chair at the table and moved another close to her.

"I'm saying," he began, "that I was wrong. Peggy's yours and should have been from the beginning. I told George to stop advertising for families right after we met Mr. and Mrs. Dobbs.''

He was glad Peggy was sleeping in the next room. It kept Jane from yelling at him. Her voice still conveyed her anger. ''That was more than a week ago, Adam.''

''Johnny was the problem by then,'' he said. ''I won't go into detail, but there was an incident that gave me serious doubts about him.''

''Johnny? He's just a boy like any other.''

Adam had to laugh at her assessment. ''No, I think he's a little unusual. But he and I have come to an understanding.''

''You said 'bargains' before. Are you going to tell me?''

''Yes, I need to do that.'' Adam found himself smiling again. ''But first I want to ask you to marry me.''

She looked a little more stunned than he had expected. He wasn't sure if that was good or bad.

''You want to marry me? Even after I said I didn't trust you?''

''I'm hoping you'll learn to trust me.''

''I do, Adam. I was wrong before, and my grandmother lied to me.'' She waved her hands in front of her. ''Never mind that. Why do you want to marry me?''

''For the house, of course.'' He grabbed her hand, laughing. ''I'm teasing. Jane, I love you. I need to be able to come home to you.''

Tears came to her eyes, and he felt a wave of alarm. He had messed this up before; he didn't want to do it again.

He was immensely relieved when she threw herself across the small space between them. He treated himself to a kiss while he had her on his lap. She was a willing participant and the kiss turned slow and seductive. It almost made him forget what else he wanted to tell her.

When she finally sat back she was breathless. She smiled a little shyly. He thought she was beautiful. "I suppose I should admit," she whispered, "that I've been in love with you for quite a while, too."

He grinned. "Yeah, I know."

She opened her mouth in mock outrage. "How would you know that?"

"Johnny told me. My marrying you was one of the bargains we struck." Her outrage was starting to look real. He added quickly, "I had already decided to ask you at the earliest opportunity. Your greeting tonight was very encouraging. Feel free to throw yourself at me anytime you want."

She chewed on her lower lip. "You better tell me all the bargains."

He tore his eyes away from her tempting lips. "His first request was that I spend the night here to keep Peggy safe and to keep you from worrying. In exchange he's never going to steal again, which will be hard on him since he's convinced he's quite good at it."

"Steal. When did he ever steal anything?"

Adam scratched his cheek, which was starting to feel a little rough. "That's the second thing. I'm not supposed to tell you."

"And that's when you struck a bargain to marry me?"

Adam laughed. "Johnny thought if I spent the night, it would be the right thing to do."

"Oh, but...." He watched her cheeks turn pink, enjoying every second of it. "He's just a boy," she said, but she looked toward the parlor as if she wasn't so sure.

"He's had to grow up too fast. He doesn't want you to get the reputation his mother has."

"Has? He's an orphan." She glanced again toward the parlor, probably thinking, as Adam did, that there was a lot yet to learn about Johnny.

Adam shook his head. "He overheard his mother and her boyfriend plan to leave Peggy on a busy street across town. They were going to keep Johnny because his job...and other activities were bringing in a few cents. He took his sister and ran."

Adam watched Jane's face as she tried to imagine what the children had been through. Of course, Peggy's early behavior had already given her a few clues.

But they had strayed from the subject, and he didn't have his answer yet. "So. Will you marry me?"

She brought her attention back to him and a smile

slowly spread across her face. "I want to sleep on it."

"Sleep on it?"

Jane watched Adam's handsome face register bewilderment, as if he thought she might turn him down. She took his face between her hands, feeling uncommonly bold, and whispered mere inches from his lips, "Let's sleep on it."

Realization dawned slowly and quite readably. He took her lips in a quick kiss and pulled her to her feet.

A hand on his chest stopped him from kissing her again. "Is it all right to leave Peggy?"

"She's fine," he assured her.

One strong arm wrapped possessively around Jane's waist as he turned down the wick on the lamp. He paused in the doorway to the dining room. "I should go home and shave."

Jane bit back a giggle. "I think I can stand it just this once." She brushed a hand across his very tempting jaw, then stood on her toes to plant a kiss there.

He hustled her across the dining room, then slowed to a quieter pace as they entered the hall and tiptoed past the parlor. Jane opened the door to her bedroom and invited Adam inside, feeling her heart skip when she heard the door latch shut.

She slipped her arms around his waist and lifted her face to his, knowing he'd find her lips in the dark. She opened her mouth and let her tongue duel with his, surprised at her boldness, yet thrilled by it as well. His lips left hers and trailed across her jaw, down her neck and lower, where at least three buttons on her bodice had mysteriously come loose.

Thinking to return the favor, she tried to open his shirt. Her fingers were trembling. He wasn't fully cooperating, either, his interest being centered on her cleavage. A collar button clattered to the floor. He wasn't distracted in the least. Jane imagined a future with collar buttons scattered in every room of the house.

He raised his head finally. "Light a lamp," he whispered.

"We can find the collar button later," she said, finding she could make much better progress on his shirt when he wasn't kissing her.

"Collar button?" He reached up and sent another skittering across the floor. "I want to see you."

Pleased with the notion, she lit the lamp on the stand beside the bed. He stood a few feet away, looking slightly disheveled. Of course, she wasn't any better. She looked down, drawing the edges of her bodice together, feeling shy in the pale light.

He crossed the distance between them slowly, making her body quiver with anticipation. "Am I really lucky enough to call you mine?" he whispered.

He didn't give her a chance to answer, though. He distracted her with his lips and his hands. Her clothes were in even more disorder, and her knees were weak when he spoke again.

"I want to go slowly this time, Jane, but I find myself too impatient." His fingers were untying the ribbons at the waist of her petticoats as he talked. They all dropped to a heap on the floor.

"We can go slowly next time," she said, equally eager to lose all the barriers that were between them. She drew his face down to hers for another hungry kiss. In short order, he lifted her onto the bed and settled down beside her, leaving all their clothes behind.

He pulled her up against him, and she reveled in the touch of his warm, strong body. She'd had no idea how much her skin would like the feel of his.

"I love you, Jane," he whispered. He rolled her onto her back and braced himself above her.

"I love you, too," she said, pulling him closer. A moment later she wasn't sure if she had spoken aloud or merely said the words in her head. She said them again, just in case. "I love you."

It came out a sigh that brought a decidedly arrogant chuckle to her ears. He was feeling very pleased at reducing her to jelly. "I don't know if that's your brain or your body talking, but I'll accept it either way," he said.

She wanted to object, to assure him that she truly loved him, but what he was doing was too distracting. In moments she was beyond rational thought. Her entire world was Adam. She clung to him, muffling her cries against his shoulder as she gave herself up to sensations alone—sensations, release and the blissful afterglow.

Then sleep, followed as promised by a slower, gentler uniting in the middle of the night.

Jane woke to find Adam gone. Her old fears rose up, and she felt a moment of panic. No. She wouldn't believe that he had used her and left her. The thought that he had been called away on a medical emergency wasn't reassuring. Had someone come for him while he was sleeping in her house? But no. That wasn't possible, either. She would have heard someone at her door.

By the time she was up and dressed, she was sure he had slipped back to his own house before dawn, to save her reputation, though the possibility that Peggy had worsened had her hurrying to the kitchen. Peggy was sleeping soundly, the kitten at her feet.

Jane started breakfast as quietly as possible, hoping, praying, that Adam would arrive soon—properly, of course, but soon. She didn't think she could stand waiting through another day like the one before.

Johnny came in a few minutes later. He looked in on his sister, then sat in the kitchen watching Jane. "Why ain't Dr. Hart still here?"

"He went home early this morning. I'm sure he'll be back soon." She didn't sound as certain as she had intended to.

"Did him and you have a little talk?"

She turned and tried to give the boy a severe look. It was spoiled, she was sure, by the fact that she wanted to grin. "I understand you were playing matchmaker," she said. "You should learn to mind your own business."

"This is my business," he declared. "I'm tryin' to fix up a good home for Peggy."

Jane had no answer for that and was saved from trying to think of one when she heard the front door open. And voices. She stepped into the dining room and greeted Adam and George.

"You're likely to catch the flu if you eat with us, George," she said.

"I'm going up to see Ferris, anyway. I don't see how eating with you'll matter after that."

"I got George up early to talk business," Adam explained. "I invited him to join us. He needs to talk to you."

Jane was curious, but she needed to get back to her stove. She instructed Johnny to set the table in the dining room, and brought the food out as quickly as she could. George, predictably, wanted to eat before there was any talk of business.

Adam kept tossing her looks that spoke eloquently of what they had shared the night before. She hoped Johnny wasn't reading them so easily. Or George. Lord. When she had made her wanton suggestion, she hadn't considered the morning after.

"All right," George said finally, setting his plate

aside and drawing a sheaf of papers from the empty chair beside him. "Adam's come up with a proposition, but I wanted to clear it with you before I did anything else."

Propositon? Jane glanced at Adam, only to have him wink at her. As if that explained everything.

George began spouting numbers—the amount of money still due on the house, the money in Adam's fund, the rent paid each month on the house next door. Jane was barely following, except to guess that Adam was getting the house. Long ingrained fears crept into her consciousness. She couldn't have been wrong, could she? He wasn't just after the house?

Peggy came dragging in, rubbing her eyes. Jane scooted her chair away from the table and picked the little girl up, trying to listen to George.

"Peggy bad," the child lamented.

"Does Peggy feel bad?" Jane cuddled her closer, certain she wasn't as hot as she had been the day before.

Johnny came to stand beside Jane's chair, handing Peggy a biscuit. Peggy took it, nibbled on a corner, then searched the front of her nightgown for a pocket.

"You don't have to save food no more," Johnny told her. He took the biscuit back and set it on the table. When Peggy reached for him, he lifted her and carried her around the room for a couple of minutes.

He walked close to Adam, and Peggy stretched

her arms toward him. "I can't make you feel any better than Johnny can," Adam said, but he took her anyway.

"So what it comes down to," George said, "is we extend the loan and put the little house back on the market. With the new smaller payments, you can have title to this house in six months."

"There's only one hitch that I can see," Adam said. "If Jane's going to quit taking in boarders and I'm moving in instead, the lady has to agree to marry me. She hasn't done that yet."

George chuckled, but Johnny looked truly shocked.

"Why, Dr. Hart, I've considered your proposal...overnight." She wished her cheeks weren't growing hot. "I believe I'll consent."

"Does that mean yes?" Johnny asked.

"Yep. It means you get first pick of the rooms upstairs, just like I promised," Adam said. Johnny spun around, heading for the stairs. "Don't bother Ferris," he called after him.

"What else did you promise?"

"At least two more little brothers or sisters," Adam said with a grin, adding, "so you won't miss the boarders."

George wasn't even pretending not to listen. He was checking figures, chuckling away.

"Oh, one more thing," Adam said, adjusting Peggy so he could reach across the table to tap the paper in front of George. "Put the house in Jane's name. She's always wanted a home. All I need is her heart."

* * * * *

Author's Note

Between 1850 and 1920 at least two hundred thousand children were relocated by the Children's Aid Society of New York and other agencies. In the earliest days, children were moved from the city to outlying rural communities. Later they were moved farther and farther west. While Clyde, Kansas, was the destination of at least one of these orphan trains, it is very unlikely that it would have arrived as early as the setting of this book. However, I wanted to set my story at a time in Clyde's history when the hiring of a doctor the way it occurred here would have been most credible. I would like to thank the reader for allowing me to indulge in this bit of literary license.

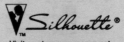

Come escape with Harlequin's new

Series Sampler

Four great full-length Harlequin novels bound together in one fabulous volume and at an unbelievable price.

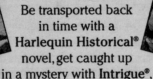

Be transported back in time with a Harlequin Historical® novel, get caught up in a mystery with Intrigue®, be tempted by a hot, sizzling romance with Harlequin Temptation®, or just enjoy a down-home all-American read with American Romance®.

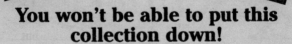

You won't be able to put this collection down!

On sale February 2000 at your favorite retail outlet.

HARLEQUIN®
Makes any time special ™

Visit us at www.romance.net   PHESC